GREEN ICE

M. R. ROSE

GREEN ICE

To Paul
Best wishes
M. R. Rose.

t₂

Troubador Publishing Ltd
9 De Montfort Mews
Leicester LE1 7FW, UK
Tel: (+44) 116 255 9311 / 9312
Email: books@troubador.co.uk
Web: www.troubador.co.uk/matador

ISBN 10: 1-905886-36-5
ISBN 13: 978-1-905886-36-4

Typeset in 11pt Stempel Garamond by Troubador Publishing Ltd, Leicester, UK
Printed in the UK by The Cromwell Press Ltd, Trowbridge, Wilts, UK

T2 is an imprint of Troubador Publishing Ltd

*Green Ice
is for
Rob and Will
with love*

Contents

The Meteorite

1

I was sitting in front of the TV rubbing my bruises and feeling a bit sorry for myself when my mobile 'phone rang. It was Jun Mo, my friend from school asking if I wanted to meet him at the cinema to see the latest film.

'When?' I asked, still a bit down after the run-in with my brother Luke. I didn't want to admit that my legs and the tops of my arms were hurting like hell where Luke had punched me. He called it play fighting, but he was four years older than me and at seventeen, packed a fairly hefty punch.

'Film starts at half past three,' Jun Mo said in his cool South Korean accent. 'You want to go? I've already asked Charlotte.'

I glanced at the rubbish I'd been watching on the TV and said, 'Yeah, why not. I'll see you there.'

Turning off the Saturday afternoon sports programme, I went into the kitchen to see if I could wheedle a lift out of my mum. I was quite capable of walking to the station and getting a train into

Guildford, but it was much easier to scrounge a lift off my mum or dad.

Mum was lying on the kitchen floor doing sit ups. I'd forgotten she was in the middle of a training programme. She'd put her name down to join some sort of charity walk through Africa and was jogging or working out whenever she wasn't cooking dinner or driving me or Luke around.

Deciding I'd better not disturb her, I walked into the garage and found Dad who had just finished putting the tools away in his tool box. He closed the lid of the box with a snap and looked up. 'Hi, William,' he said. 'What are you up to? Done all your homework yet?'

Dad is the only person who still calls me William. My name is Will, and has been for the last two years. He's also really annoying about checking my homework. Even Mum only asks once or twice at the weekend about what homework I've got and seems happy if I tell her it's all under control. Dad asks me every time he sees me.

'I'm doing it tomorrow, Dad,' I said, trying not to sound frustrated with him because I really wanted that lift. 'You know I always do it Sunday afternoon.'

'You'd do better to get it out of the way earlier in the weekend,' he said. 'Then you could relax on Sunday.'

'I can't do it today anyway; Jun Mo has asked me to go with him and Charlotte to the cinema.'

'Oh yes? And how are you getting there?'

'Actually, I was hoping you might give me a lift.'

2

I think he would have said no, only at that minute we both noticed a blast of rain hitting the garage window. It had only been drizzling a bit earlier, but now great raindrops were lashing down outside, making puddles in the dips on the gravel drive.

'Okay,' he said. 'It is rather wet out there. Have you asked Mum if it's alright to go?'

He went into the house to change out of the dreaded tracksuit he'd been working in, and I followed him through the kitchen where Mum was now doing hamstring leg stretches against the cereal cupboard.

I told her about the cinema and she seemed to think it was a good idea.

'Why don't you ask Jun Mo back here for a sleepover afterwards?' she suggested. 'Dad and I are going out this evening and he will be company for you.'

'Will Luke be in?' I asked anxiously.

'Only for a little while,' Mum said. 'I think he's going out with his friends later on, so he won't be here to keep you company.'

'Great, I'll ring Jun Mo back and ask him,' I said. I'd never told Mum or Dad where the bruises on my legs and arms came from. Luke never did play fighting in front of them as he knew he'd be in big trouble. When he did anything really bad like shooting holes in the playroom light shade with his Bibi gun, they stopped his lifts or weekly allowance. If I told on him he'd probably kill me.

'What about Charlotte?' I asked. 'Can she come too?'

'Well, she'll have to sleep in the guest room, not on the sofa bed in the playroom with you boys. I'll give her mother a ring and see what she says.'

And that's how the evening started; nice and normal.

The film, as it turned out, wasn't up to much, but we ate our way through three boxes of sweet popcorn and a shared bag of sweets, not to mention the multi coloured Ice Blasts we'd all bought with our pocket money.

Dad collected us and we settled down in the old playroom to watch a DVD he'd rented to keep us quiet while he and Mum went out.

'We'll be late back,' Mum said as she came to say goodbye. 'Be good!'

As soon as they'd gone, Luke stuck his head round the playroom door. 'Hi you lot,' he said. I noticed he'd got a wicked glint in his eye and wondered what he was going to do to me and my friends. I watched him suspiciously as he went into the garage and I heard cupboard doors opening and closing in there.

'What's he doing?' Jun Mo asked. Jun Mo, like all my friends thought Luke was really cool. They didn't have to live with him.

Jun Mo's question was answered when Luke reappeared clutching a six pack of Dad's lagers, left over from the last barbecue.

'I'm off out with my mates,' he told us. 'You lot better not tell anyone I took these.'

Neither Jun Mo, nor Charlotte said anything. They knew I wouldn't dare tell on my brother and I could tell they were in awe of him.

We watched the DVD, cooked and ate a pizza Mum had left in the freezer for us, then watched another film on the TV. I was about to go to the freezer again to get some ice for our cokes as the room was getting warm again now the rain had stopped, and then I remembered the ice trays were empty.

Sitting back down again, I sipped at the tepid drink and grimaced…and that's when it happened.

One minute everything was quiet and dark outside the open window, because even though it was summer, it was gone midnight by then and pitch black in the garden. The next, we heard a sort of whistling sound like a firework rocket whooshing upwards, and then there was a crashing, breaking noise and a terrific thud. The room actually shook, and we looked at each other, muted the TV and held our breath to listen.

Nothing else happened for a minute, and then the cat flap slapped open and Brutus, our ginger cat came flying through it into the playroom with his fur on end and his tail fluffed out like a loo brush.

'Crickey, Brutus,' I said in my best Australian accent, breaking the sudden shocked silence. 'Ruddy 'ell, you got a croc after you or something, mate?'

Charlotte giggled nervously and reached out to stroke the terrified cat.

Brutus's name was a bit of a joke. We'd named

the poor scruffy little kitten Brutus when we'd first got him because the name seemed larger than life, and Brutus was a small stringy creature who was scared of just about everything.

'What was that?' Jun Mo asked; his eyes wider than I'd ever seen them. 'That was one heck of a big bang.'

'I'm scared,' whispered Charlotte, pulling the cat onto her lap. 'What do you think it was?'

They were both looking at me as I rested my drink back down on the old kitchen chair we used as a coffee table. I wondered if perhaps Luke had come back and let a firework off in the garden, but that still didn't account for the crashing noise or the fact that the whole room had shaken like there'd been an earthquake or something.

'I think we'd better go and look,' I said, standing up and going to the window. I peered out into the blackness, but there was nothing to see.

'Should we go outside?' Jun Mo asked.

'You go,' said Charlotte, looking at me. 'It's your house, after all.'

'We'll all go,' I said decisively. 'There's safety in numbers, or so my parents are always telling me.'

We crept out of the playroom, through the kitchen and stood peering out through the toughened glass of the back door into the dark night.

'I can't see anything,' said Charlotte in a small voice. 'Perhaps we imagined it after watching that scary movie.'

'Brutus didn't see the movie,' Jun Mo pointed

out. 'And he seemed very scared.'

'I think we'd better go outside and look properly,' I said with more braveness than I actually felt. Grabbing my torch from a drawer on the way through the kitchen, I glanced round at my two companions as I unlocked the kitchen door and opened it a fraction. Jun Mo was small and stocky; his dark head only coming to the middle of my chest, but the set of his broad shoulders and his expression was one of fierce determination. Charlotte, who was nearly as tall as me was hanging back.

'Do we have to?' she said.

I was halfway out of the door by then, with Jun Mo at my heels. Charlotte followed us more slowly.

'The crashing we heard sounded like breaking wood,' I whispered over my shoulder. 'Let's see if a firework exploded in the shed or something.'

We crept down the garden path towards the shed, following the circle of yellow light that I shone ahead of us onto the concrete.

The shed was at the end of the garden, nestling up against a high stone, ivy covered wall, which separated our garden from the neighbour's. No one had used the shed in years since the roof had grown leaky and the incoming rain had turned Dad's garden tools to rust, forcing him to move them to the garage.

'No sign of flames,' I whispered.

'We going in?' Jun Mo hissed at my elbow.

Reaching out a trembling hand I pushed slowly, creakily at the shed door until it was fully open; then I shone the beam of the torch inside. What we saw in the wavering torch light simply took our breath away.

There, in the middle of the crater it had made in the dirt floor sat a great gleaming ball of gritty looking ice.

'Blimey,' I breathed, stepping inside the shed for a closer look. 'What on *earth* is that?'

Delta Aquarids

2

The three of us stood gawping open mouthed at the thing before us.

'It looks like a huge dirty snowball,' Charlotte whispered. 'But it's nearly the end of July; so how did it get here?'

Shining the beam of light upwards we all gasped in unison. There above our heads gaped a great jagged hole in the shed roof.

'It's space ice,' breathed Jun Mo in hushed tones. 'It's come from the sky!'

'Wow,' I said, walking round the huge ice ball and playing the torch over it, 'Look at the hole it's made in the floor!'

'Do you think it's safe?' Charlotte asked nervously as I reached out my hand to touch it. 'I mean, if it's from space it might be dangerous.'

I pulled back my hand and we all stared at the huge snowball for a few moments, considering what to do next.

'Maybe it's part of a comet,' Charlotte said from where she was still standing well back by the door.

'I read that comets are made up of dust and rocks and are held together by ice and frozen gas.'

'How did it get here?' Jun Mo said getting as close to the thing as possible without actually touching it and peering closely at it. 'Comets are supposed to stay in space.'

'Maybe it's a meteorite then,' Charlotte said. 'Meteorites fall to Earth don't they?'

'I know!' I said suddenly. 'Let's turn on the news channel and see if there's anything on there about a comet passing through our orbit. Maybe a bit broke off and got pulled into Earth's gravity or something.'

'Yeah, okay clever clogs,' Charlotte said. She liked to tease me whenever I said anything smart, though I could hear from her voice she was relieved at the excuse to go back into the safety of the house.

We backed out of the shed and Jun Mo pulled the door closed behind us as we hurried up the path towards the house. I glanced up at the dark outlines of the houses on either side of ours but no lights had come on: obviously the noise hadn't woken the neighbours.

In the playroom I turned the TV back on and ran through the channels until I came to a 24 hour news station, then the three of us sat staring hopefully at the flickering screen. There were a couple of reports about the usual boring government things and talk of some un-seasonal weather around the world, and then a picture of a night sky speckled with glowing lights.

'And, to finish tonight's programme, we have reports just coming in about the Delta Aquarids,' said the news reader. 'Apparently this strong meteor shower gives a splendid show in our night skies every year at this time, peaking in the next few days on July 28th. According to the British Astronomical Association this year is particularly interesting, so to all you budding astronomy enthusiasts we say; get out there with your telescopes and enjoy the show.'

We watched for another few minutes to see if there was anything more about it, but even after running through the different channels again, we couldn't find anything else.

Charlotte yawned and even Jun Mo had begun to look tired, but I wasn't having any of it. 'Come on you two!' I said. 'This is the most amazing thing that's ever happened around here and I'm not just going to bed and forgetting all about it. I think we should go and have another look at our meteor.'

'It's a meteorite,' Charlotte corrected me. 'It's only a meteor while it's still in the atmosphere. If a meteor falls to earth it's called a meteor*ite*.'

'Yeah, whatever,' I said. 'Come on then you two.'

The meteorite or whatever it was, looked smaller somehow when we shone the torch on it this time.

'Do you think it's melting?' I asked anxiously.

'Maybe,' Jun Mo said, nodding. 'It's very wet.'

Jun Mo was right. Not only was the huge snowy mass getting smaller by the second, its surface was glistening with melted water or gas or whatever it was made of.

'Here,' I said, thrusting the torch at Jun Mo,

'Keep an eye on it, will you? I'm going to find something to hack a bit off it with. No one will believe us if it disappears altogether, will they?'

Leaving Jun Mo and a nervous Charlotte watching our extraordinary find I hurried through the house to the garage, where I grabbed up the tool box I'd seen Dad putting away earlier and rummaged through it. There was a saw, a hammer and a chisel. I took all three and headed back through the house and down the garden to find Jun Mo and Charlotte standing just inside the shed looking worried.

'It's melting really fast,' Charlotte said as I approached with the tools.

'Hey, give them to me,' Jun Mo said. Grabbing the hammer and chisel from me and going towards the meteorite, he stood for a moment with his head on one side as if choosing the best spot to hit it. He made a decision quickly and placed the chisel against one rounded side of the ball. As soon as it was in place, he whacked it with the hammer, splitting a chunk off the side with a creaking, splintering sound.

We peered at the place he'd hit, trying to see if the inside of the meteorite was any different from the outside, but it all looked much the same: just dirty ice and rocks all stuck together.

'What are we going to put it in?' Charlotte said from the doorway. 'It'll melt even quicker now we've split it.'

'I'll go and get some of Mum's freezer bags,' I said, and I hurried off, leaving them with the meteorite again.

There was a saying Mum liked to use when she was rushing about the place and things kept going wrong, 'more haste less speed,' she liked to mutter. Well now I knew what she meant. As I wrenched open the drawer where I thought she kept the freezer bags, the drawer knob came off in my hand.

'Damn!' I said, trying to push it back into place. I was so worried the meteorite would disappear before I could get any of it into the freezer, I grabbed at the roll of bags too fast and the whole roll flew out of my hands, flopped out of the box and unravelled across the floor making a plastic footpath across the kitchen. Dropping the drawer knob I dived at the roll just before it vanished under the freezer and ripped off a handful of bags.

Hurrying back down the garden, I arrived at the shed just as Jun Mo raised the hammer for what looked to be the third or fourth time. Lumps of dirty grey ice lay round the main ball like jagged babies lying round their mother.

'Quick!' I said to Charlotte, thrusting a couple of bags at her. 'Put the bits in the bags before they melt any more.'

Jun Mo paused with his hammering as Charlotte and I scooped up handfuls of the ice and dropped them into the bags.

'You want more?' he asked.

'Yes, as much as we can get,' I told him. 'I'll go and put these in the freezer, but you just keep chopping bits off.'

Back at the house, I knelt before the freezer,

opened it and pulled out a carton of ice cream and some frozen peas, then hid the bags of meteorite ice at the back. I was just putting the ice cream back in when I heard a noise behind me, and I looked up sharply.

'So, little bro', what are you up to then?'

'Oh, it's you,' I said, my heart pounding. 'I thought you were out with your mates.'

The last thing I wanted was for Luke to find our meteorite. He'd probably start chucking it round the garden, or worse still, I could imagine him throwing it over next door's fence or something.

'Where are your mates then, squib? They got bored with you and gone home?'

'No, we're um…playing hide and seek.' I said, trying to think of something quickly.

'You're a bit old for that aren't you? And anyway I don't suppose you'll find them in the freezer,' he said with a laugh.

Glancing up at him, I realised he was in one of his 'good moods', the weird and unpredictable moods he got in after he'd had a few beers.

'I don't s'pose they're hiding in with the frozen peas,' he continued, giving me a playful push so that I lost my balance where I'd been squatting by the freezer on my heels and fell over backwards. 'Bit old to be playing games like that aren't you Billy?'

'Yeah, well, I'd better find them before Mum and Dad get home,' I said, scrambling to my feet.

'Do you want me to help you?'

'No, leave us alone will you, Luke? They're my friends.'

'Don't tell me you've murdered them and chopped them up and put their dismembered bodies in the freezer?' he said with a suspicious grin. 'You look guilty as hell little bro'.'

'Here,' I said, dragging out some fluff covered sweets from my pocket. 'You can have these if you want.'

His eyes narrowed suspiciously. 'Now I know you're up to something,' he said. 'What did you put in there, eh?'

'Nothing!'

'Oh, yeah? Well how come I don't believe you?'

And he pushed past me, opened the freezer door and started rummaging around in the shelves.

'Stop it!' I shouted at him. 'Mum will be really cross if we leave the freezer open, everything will defrost!'

'Hey, you,' said a voice behind us. Luke and I both turned to see Jun Mo standing there with Charlotte close behind him.

'Where have you been?' Jun Mo asked. 'We've been waiting for you.'

'There,' I said to Luke. 'I told you we were playing hide and seek.'

'Do what?' Jun Mo asked.

Charlotte gave him a dig with her elbow and flashed him a knowing look, 'Hide and seek, you know; the game.'

Luke looked from one of us to the other, then laughed and gave me a poke in the ribs. 'So what were you doing in the freezer if you were supposed to be finding them?' he inquired.

'He was getting us ice for our drinks,' Charlotte put in. 'The cokes were really warm and nasty. We were going to have them when he'd…er…found us.'

I smiled in relief. Charlotte and Jun Mo had obviously heard Luke return and left the meteorite safely in the shed where he wouldn't think of looking. And they were playing along with my 'hide and seek' story nicely.

'Funny ice,' said Luke suddenly, reaching sideways to pull out one of the bags I had so carefully hidden only moments ago and holding it up to the light, 'looks a bit grubby to me.'

'There's nothing wrong with it,' Charlotte said bravely.

Luke got up and went into the playroom, holding the bag of ice.

As soon as he was out of earshot, I grabbed Jun Mo's shoulder. 'What have you done with the rest of it?' I hissed.

'It's still in the shed,' he whispered back. 'We shut the door and came in when we heard Luke.'

'He mustn't find it,' I said urgently. 'He'll just destroy it, and we found it.'

Charlotte nodded. 'I won't tell him,' she whispered.

'Here you go then,' Luke said from the doorway. 'Here's your nice ice coke, Charlotte. If there's nothing wrong with the ice, you won't mind drinking it, will you?'

Space Ice

3

We all turned to see Luke leaning against the kitchen door, looking smug. He was holding one of the glasses of coke we'd abandoned earlier when we'd heard the meteorite crashing to earth. I could just see the top of something grey sticking out of the glass.

'Yours, I think,' he said, handing the glass to Charlotte.

Charlotte went pale and backed slightly away from him, her eyes wide. 'It's not mine,' she said.

Luke crossed the kitchen and stood in front of me. 'Yours then?' he asked.

Staring at the piece of meteorite sloshing about in the glass of cola I wondered how dangerous it could possibly be. It was only dirt and ice, wasn't it? And with any luck, any germs that had been lurking in it would have got zapped with the heat of the meteorite's entry into the earth's atmosphere. I'd seen film of the Apollo landings on TV and was pretty sure things got very hot on re-entry, which is why the rockets had to have heat resistant tiles on their undersides.

I was still thinking about it, when Jun Mo stuck his hand out. 'It's mine,' he said bravely.

Charlotte and I watched as Jun Mo took the glass from my brother and put it to his lips, taking a small sip of the coke and no doubt a mouthful of the melting ice.

'Taste good, does it?' Luke asked.

'Yes,' Jun Mo said defiantly.

'Then you won't mind finishing the rest,' Luke said.

I could see Luke watching the three of us carefully. He knew we'd been up to something but he didn't know what it was. The condition of the ice was obviously puzzling him, so now he was testing his theory that we'd done something nasty to the stuff he'd found me hiding in the freezer.

Jun Mo took another gulp of the cola, but then I grabbed the drink from him and before he could stop me I took a great big mouthful and swallowed it.

'Yeah, not bad,' I said, holding the drink out to Luke. 'Want to try some?'

'Nah, think I'll pass on that one,' Luke said, peering into the scummy liquid and wrinkling his nose. 'But I'll bet Charlotte would like some though, wouldn't you Charlotte?'

Luke took the glass from my hand and thrust it at Charlotte, who stared at it gingerly.

'Go on then,' Luke said. 'You told me there's nothing wrong with it, so drink some.'

Charlotte put the glass to her lips, closed her eyes and swallowed. 'Delicious,' she announced, looking rather sick.

Luke looked from one of us to the other, still not sure what he was missing, but then he gave me a hearty slap on the back and grinned widely.

'Right, well, I'm off to my room, I've got some texts to send. Enjoy the rest of your evening, squibs.'

We listened as he stamped out of the kitchen and up the stairs. When we heard his bedroom door slam shut Charlotte threw the rest of the coke down the sink and stood looking at us in horror.

'It could be poisonous!' she exclaimed. 'We could all be dead tomorrow.'

'I feel okay,' Jun Mo said. 'Shall we go see the rest of the space ice now?'

I glanced at my watch. 'Mum and Dad should be home soon; it's gone one o'clock in the morning. We'll have to be quick if we're going to have one last try at saving some of it.'

We grabbed up the torch and headed back down the garden to the shed and Jun Mo opened the door so we could all peer inside. The meteorite was shrinking fast, the grubby water trickling down the outsides of the boulder and pooling in the crater at its base. The bits Jun Mo had already hacked off were gone, probably melted away into the dirt floor of the shed.

For the next ten minutes, we sliced and hammered at the meteorite until we'd filled four more freezer bags full of the ice slivers.

'Okay, I think that's about it,' I said straightening up. 'Mum and Dad will be home any minute, so let's get these hidden in the freezer and get to bed.'

Charlotte had just gone up to the guest room, and Jun Mo and I had climbed into our sleeping bags when we heard the sound of tyres crunching on the gravel drive at the front of the house.

'You going to tell them about space ice?' Jun Mo asked sleepily as we heard the key turn in the front door.

'Yeah...It's pretty exciting,' I said. 'Maybe we could report it to that Space Agency they mentioned on the TV...'

And suddenly, inexplicably, without the normal dozing and winding down, I was fast asleep.

In the morning I woke up with a slight headache. The sun was streaming in through the blinds making a slatted effect across the carpet, and I stared at the stripes for a while trying to remember what had happened the evening before.

'The meteorite!' I gasped as my memory returned. I turned to where Jun Mo was still snoring in his sleeping bag and shook him awake. 'Hey, Jun Mo. Did I dream it, or did we find a meteorite last night?'

'Yeah, we found space ice,' muttered Jun Mo as he pushed himself up on one elbow into a sitting position. He rubbed his hand through his sleek black hair and blinked. 'I've got brain ache.'

'So have I,' I admitted. 'You don't think it was the ice?'

'Shall we go see it?' he asked, nodding hopefully. 'See if it's still there?'

'I think we ought to wait for Charlotte.'

At that moment the playroom door pushed quietly open and Charlotte stuck her head round. Her long fair hair was tousled and she looked a bit dazed.

'Hey, you two, did I dream it, or did we find a meteorite last night?'

'We're going to look right now,' Jun Mo said, pulling himself out of his sleeping bag. 'See if it's still there.'

Charlotte was rubbing her forehead. 'I've got a bit of a headache this morning.'

Jun Mo and I glanced at each other. 'So have we,' I told her.

'You don't think it was the ice?'

I shrugged, 'It might have been. Look, clear off a minute will you? I've got to go to the bathroom and get my clothes on.'

When we were ready, the three of us crept out of the sleeping house and down the garden in the early morning sunshine. It was already quite hot and I wondered if there would be anything left of the meteorite. Opening the shed door as quietly as we could, we peered inside and then went in, standing in a row as we stared down at the deep empty crater in the shed floor.

'It's melted,' Charlotte breathed, stating the obvious. 'What a shame, I wanted to see what it looked like in the daylight.'

'It's not all gone,' I said, going and crouching by

the hole in the floor. 'Look, there are all sorts of tiny bits of rock and dust in this puddle at the bottom.'

'Let's go check the stuff in the freezer,' Jun Mo said at my shoulder. 'Maybe we should show your mother and father.'

'Yeah, if there's still some evidence, we ought to tell someone,' I agreed, excited by the thought. 'Lucky we kept some of the ice before it all melted.'

With a last look at the hole, we all trooped back to the kitchen. I opened the freezer door, moved the ice cream to one side and then gasped, rummaging more frantically under frozen peas and behind packets of ready meals. Eventually I sat back on my haunches and let out a long slow breath. 'It's not here.'

'Oh, no,' Charlotte groaned from somewhere behind me, 'Look in the sink.'

Standing up I turned and looked into the sink, my heart pounding. And there, lying crumpled beside the washing up bowl was a pile of dirty looking freezer bags...all quite empty.

Boffins

4

The loss of the ice was a disaster. Now no one would ever believe that a meteorite had crashed to Earth and that we had actually seen it and touched it.

'Damn!' I cussed angrily, looking at the empty freezer bags in dismay. 'Luke must have come down in the night and thrown them in here. Why does he always have to spoil everything?'

'There's not much point in telling your parents now, is there?' Charlotte said despondently. 'They'd never believe us.'

'There's the hole in the shed roof,' Jun Mo put in. 'That's good evidence.'

'Yeah, but with no meteorite it's hardly front page news is it?' I said. 'I can see the headlines now: Deranged teenagers find hole in shed roof and say a meteorite landed in their garden in the night. Hardly believable, is it?'

We made a pile of toast and jam and sat munching gloomily. Despite the glorious day outside, we all felt cold and a bit shivery.

'I'm freezing!' Charlotte said as she pulled a

fleece top over her head, 'Maybe there was a virus in the ice; something that's never been discovered on Earth. Of course that means there isn't a cure and then we will all be dead by tomorrow.'

'Cheerful thought,' I said. 'You'd better ring later, when you've got home and check that we're all still breathing.'

An hour later Charlotte and Jun Mo had gone home, Charlotte by car, collected by her parents and Jun Mo by train. I mooched about the place, waiting for Luke to wake up so I could call him a few choice names, while Dad put some meat in the oven for Sunday lunch and Mum went out for a run.

I toyed with the idea of telling my parents about the meteorite, but having gone outside to look at the shed I realised the hole couldn't actually be seen from the garden because it was on the other side of the roof slope, against the wall. Opening the door, I saw Dad's tools lying on the shed floor and grabbed them up. Dad would be furious that I'd taken them without asking and even more angry if I left them there to rust.

Hurrying to the garage, I slid them back into the tool box while Dad was sitting safely in the lounge reading the Sunday paper. It was as I was closing the lid that I noticed some pale-green goo sticking to the edge of the chisel, exactly where it had been in contact with the meteorite. Brushing my finger against it, I realised it was more of a watery substance with green flecks in it, than a solid stickiness, and I wiped it quickly off onto my sweatshirt, so Dad wouldn't know I'd used the chisel.

The rest of the day passed normally, if you can count an hour of maths homework as normal, or the fact that neither Mum nor Dad remembered the roast until it had shrunk to the size of a fist, and Luke and I had to fight over who got the most to eat. But I didn't care too much about the homework anyway, partly because it had been the easiest maths I had ever been set, and partly because the summer term was almost over and the long summer holidays were looming ahead of me like an adventure waiting to happen.

Even Dad was pleased that I'd done the homework so easily. He'd been quite surprised by the amount I'd got, but even more surprised by the fact I did it without any help.

'That's really complicated stuff you're doing there, William,' he said with a note of pride in his voice. 'I didn't think maths was one of your favourite subjects. Are you sure you had to do the whole chapter? It looks like an awful lot of work to me.'

'The teacher said to work for an hour, and that's what I've done,' I said.

It wasn't until Charlotte rang later that afternoon that I realised Dad had been right.

'Did you do the maths homework?' Charlotte asked me.

'Yeah, it was pip squeak,' I boasted.

'I thought so too,' she confided. 'But Will, we're not even in the top set and today I did the whole lot really easily!'

'Don't complain,' I said. 'Maybe the teacher made a mistake and set us this easy stuff.'

'I thought so too, until Mum saw what I'd done. She says it's incredible that I understood it all so well. She thinks I cheated somehow.'

'Well, it seemed easy to me, too.'

'Do you think it's something to do with the ice?' Charlotte asked nervously. 'Have we turned into a couple of boffins?'

'I don't think that's likely,' I laughed. 'But I'll go and look at Dad's crossword and see if I've suddenly become a genius, okay?'

Although I thought Charlotte was being silly, I did go and look at the crossword, and that's when I started to get really scared. It was like the answers were already written in for me. I just glanced at the clues, looked at the crossword grid, and hey presto I knew all the answers. Grabbing a pen, I tested the answers out and then sat there staring at the paper as if it had turned into some sort of monster. Every answer fitted perfectly into the grid. I *was* a genius. Crikey, mate, I thought.

The 'phone rang then and it was Jun Mo on the line.

'Hey you,' he said.

'Hi,' I answered, 'You done the maths homework yet?'

'That's what I'm ringing for,' he said hesitantly. 'You find the homework easy?'

I filled Jun Mo in on what I had discovered about being able to do the maths and the crossword and he made weird noises at the other end of the line that I took to be excitement.

'A very strange thing happened on my way home on the train too,' he said breathlessly. 'Some teenagers tried to take my mobile 'phone. I said "No, get your own 'phone," and they tried to push me. But I wouldn't push! I just stayed upright and one boy said, "Okay you want to play the tough guy," and he got out a knife! I was very scared, but when he shoved the knife at me, it seemed to move so slowly I was able to knock it out of his hand! It felt like I was very strong, very quick and very clever.'

'Crikey,' I said in the Australian accent I'd learned off that programme where the presenter wrestled crocs and handled snakes without seeming to get hurt. 'Ruddy 'ell, mate, you sound like a regular Crocodile Dundee.'

But although I was making light of things, my mind was busy working overtime. 'Do you think it was the ice?' I said lowering my voice as Dad walked past. 'Charlotte thinks it was. Do you think it's because we drank some of it in that coke?'

'Maybe,' he said. 'Pity Luke threw the rest away.'

'Yeah,' I groaned. 'We could have had it analysed or something!'

A shout from behind me had me looking over my shoulder. I turned to see Dad holding the paper up to show Mum. 'You did my crossword!' he accused her. 'You know I always do the crossword on a Sunday afternoon.'

'It wasn't me,' she said in a surprised voice. 'I wouldn't waste my time on such things. You know I'd rather be training than doing crosswords.'

'Well who did it then?' he demanded.

They both turned to look at me where I stood with the 'phone pressed to my ear. I felt myself flush guiltily, but shrugged, 'Maybe someone in the newsagents did it before they delivered the paper.'

'You told a lie to your parents!' Jun Mo accused from the other end of the 'phone. 'You must always respect your parents.'

After checking that Mum and Dad were no longer looking in my direction, I lowered my voice. 'I didn't lie, exactly,' I said. 'I just suggested it as a possibility. They're never going to believe *I* did it are they?'

'What are we going to do?' he asked, and I knew he wasn't still talking about the crossword.

'Well,' I said, my spirits brightening, 'It's our school sports day tomorrow isn't it? Maybe we could use a little of this good fortune to our advantage.'

Monday dawned bright and sunny and I set off for school with a bounce in my step. We only had three lessons before the sports day began, and one of them was maths. With my perfect maths homework carefully stowed in my school bag, I arrived for registration feeling pretty darned pleased with myself.

Jun Mo grinned when he saw me and gave me the thumbs up. We'd had a bit of a problem when he'd joined the school from Korea two years ago, because he didn't understand English and he was always getting the gestures wrong. It had remained a joke between us that the first time he'd greeted me with what he'd thought was a friendly gesture he'd got a detention from the head of year. Now we occasionally made inappropriate gestures just for the fun of it, but I was relieved he wasn't mucking about now.

Our form teacher Mr Stewart was also our maths teacher, so we left our homework on his desk as we all filed out into the corridor to go to the humanities block for our history class. As we passed the Head Master's office I spotted a tall thin man in a business suit standing outside the office door. He peered closely at us all as we trooped past, and although I quickly dropped my gaze, I had the feeling his eyes were boring into the back of my head as I walked away from him.

As soon as we'd rounded the corner Jun Mo grabbed my arm excitedly. 'You see that man?' he hissed. 'He had a gun under his jacket.'

'Don't be daft Jun Mo,' I laughed. 'I admit he looked a bit odd, but I didn't see any gun.'

'You don't need to see a gun to know it is there,' Jun Mo insisted, 'and he had a gun, I'm sure of it.'

'People in England don't walk around carrying guns,' I assured him. 'Even most of the police don't carry them. He was just some stupid school inspector or something.'

Jun Mo stuck out his square jaw in the stubborn way I'd seen in the past, and although he didn't say anything else about it, I knew he thought he'd been right about the gun. As we settled in our chairs in the history classroom I wondered fleetingly if I should have told a teacher about Jun Mo's suspicions. After all, there had been a massacre in schools both here and in America and Russia in the recent past.

But I forgot all about the man when the lesson began. Mrs Turner was telling us that she was going to test us on the Kings and Queens of England, from William the Conqueror to the present day. We'd been studying the subject all term, she reminded us; so we ought to be very good by now. Sighing, I prepared myself to be in trouble. Although I found history interesting, I simply couldn't remember the order of Kings and Queens, there were so many of them. My grandmother had even tried teaching me a verse once, which included the nickname of every monarch in the order they reigned, but even she had given up when I couldn't remember it.

'You have twenty minutes to write down the complete list,' Mrs Turner was telling us. 'You don't need to include dates on this occasion, but please try to get the Kings and Queens in order! Oh, and by the way,' she continued. 'The head has asked me to tell you that a certain gentleman from the Space Agency will be visiting us today to talk about the meteor shower you have probably heard about on the news. He will visit each classroom in turn, and we expect you all to be on your very best behaviour while he is here.'

Jun Mo was nudging me and giving me knowing glances and I must admit I was getting a tingling feeling down my spine as I picked up my pen. A man from the Space Agency, here in our school the very day after we'd discovered a lump of space ice in my back garden? Was it just a coincidence? I had the horrible feeling it might be a lot more than that; especially if Jun Mo was right and the man *was* carrying a gun.

The Man from the Space Agency

5

The history test was going remarkably well. Despite the fact that half my mind was occupied with the man from the Space Agency, the other half seemed to be excelling itself.

It had been years since my grandma had tried to teach me the verse about the Kings and Queens and yet suddenly I found I knew it as clearly as I knew my own name. I began to write, sure that at last I'd get a merit from Mrs Turner and maybe some respect from the rest of the class.

I started with William the Conqueror and gave shortened names for the rest of the monarchs, but they were all there...and in order.

Willie, Willie, Harry, Ste,

Harry, Dick, John, Harry three,

One, two, three Edwards, Richard two

Harry four, five, six then who?

Edwards four, five, Dick the bad, Harry's twain and Ned the lad,

Mary, Bessie, James the vain, Charlie, Charlie, James again,

William and Mary, Anna Gloria,
Four Georges, William and Victoria!
Edward, George, Edward, George, Elizabeth.

I put my pen down with a grin and looked back at the verse. If read like a poem it all rhymed beautifully, and as Grandma had put the whole thing to the tune of 'Twinkle Twinkle Little Star' which was a pretty catchy tune for the five or six year old I had been at the time, I couldn't understand why I hadn't been able to learn it before.

'Will, should I assume from your grin that you have already finished the work?' Mrs Turner's voice boomed across the classroom.

'Yes Miss,' I said.

She had a look on her face that said quite clearly that she didn't believe me. 'Perhaps you'd like to come to the front of the classroom and read your work out to the rest of the class then?' she said.

Pushing back my chair as noisily as possible, I sauntered to the front of the class, feeling pretty smug.

'Well, kindly read what you have written,' she said.

I took a deep breath, thinking of the tune in my head. 'Willie, Willie, Harry, Ste, Harry, Dick, John, Harry three,' I said loudly. 'One, two, three Edwards, Richard two, Harry four, five, six, then who? Edwards four, five, Dick the bad, Harry's twain and Ned the lad. Mary, Bessie, James the vain, Charlie, Charlie, James again. William and Mary, Anna Gloria, four Georges, William and Victoria.

Edward, George, Edward George, Elizabeth.'

I looked round the classroom to see all eyes upon me in astonishment. At last I'd showed them all, I thought.

'And where may I ask did you learn that?' Mrs Turner asked quietly.

'My grandma taught it to me,' I said proudly.

'So,' Mrs Turner continued in an icy voice, 'am I to understand that after a whole school year of my lessons, the best you can do is recite a verse your granny taught you?'

The rest of the class sniggered, and I reeled back almost as if Mrs Turner had slapped me in the face.

'It's all the kings and queens in order,' I said indignantly. 'It's what you asked for.'

'Yes, well,' Mrs Turner huffed. 'Maybe it is, but it's not what I taught you, is it? Yes?'

I turned to see that Charlotte had her hand stuck in the air.

'What do you want Charlotte?' Mrs Turner asked crisply.

'I think it's a brilliant verse, Miss,' she said. 'I've memorised it already.'

I could see the teacher struggling with her wounded pride and realised that by being clever for a change I had somehow upset her rather than impressing her. I smiled at Charlotte to thank her for her support and Mrs Turner took the look to mean that somehow we were in cahoots together.

'Well, seeing as you both have such a sudden passion for my subject, perhaps you would both like to come back at break time and write the verse out three times each on the board,' she said shortly as the bell rang. 'The rest of you may hand your papers in and go to your next lesson.'

'So much for being clever,' I grumbled to Charlotte as we walked along the corridor to our maths lesson. 'I thought she'd be pleased.'

'It's only because you'd learned it from someone other than her,' Charlotte said, 'I thought it was really cool.'

Thank goodness I hadn't mentioned the tune that went with it, I though, suppressing a sudden urge to giggle. I wasn't so sure even Charlotte would think singing nursery rhymes in my head was all that cool.

'Let's hope Mr Stewart is pleased with our maths homework, after all we learned everything we know about maths from him,' she added as we arrived outside his classroom and bundled through the door with the rest of the class.

The maths lesson went smoothly enough, but when the bell went for break, Mr Stewart called me, Charlotte and Jun Mo back just as we were heading out of the door.

'Okay, you three, what's your game?' he said, standing with his hands on his hips. 'Where did you get the answers for the homework?'

'I did it by myself, sir,' Charlotte muttered.

'And you two? I suppose you weren't together at the weekend by any chance? I can check with your parents, don't forget.'

'We were together, sir,' I answered truthfully, 'but I did the homework on my own on Sunday afternoon. My father will vouch for me.'

'Didn't find the answers on the internet, I suppose?' Mr Stewart asked.

'No sir.'

'Well, considering you have just handed in three completely perfect, completely identical pieces of work; pieces that would have taken even an A set student at least a day and a half to complete rather than the hour I asked of you, you'll excuse me if I don't believe you. I've got a good mind to give you each a lunchtime detention to think about the consequences of cheating.'

'But sir!' Jun Mo piped up. 'My father watched me work. He was very pleased I worked so hard.'

'Jun Mo, you may be able to pull the wool over your father's eyes, but it won't wash with me, do you understand?'

'Why would my father want wool on his eyes?' Jun Mo asked in a puzzled voice. 'And you wash the wool first?'

'I suppose you think you're clever, don't you?' Mr Stewart snapped, 'Well you can spend your break doing this piece of work if you're so smart.'

He thrust a work sheet into Jun Mo's hands and stalked out of the classroom leaving Jun Mo red in the face and angry.

'It's a saying,' I explained. 'Pulling the wool over someone's eyes means hoodwinking them, er... conning them. Look, we've got to go,' I said to Jun

Mo apologetically. 'Charlotte and I have the history detention.'

'I'll see you after break for science,' he said, turning away with the sheet. 'I'll try to do this real quick, okay?'

Charlotte and I hurried down the corridor leaving Jun Mo to his extra maths.

'It's not like we're cheating on purpose,' Charlotte seethed. 'If everything suddenly looks simple, it's going to be hard to get anything wrong, isn't it? I thought today was going to be great and that the teachers would be pleased with us because we see everything so clearly, but they just don't believe us do they?'

'Oh, well, let's get this history detention over with,' I said wearily. Charlotte was right of course, I had rather been looking forward to being top of the class for a change too. 'And thank you for sticking up for me by the way.'

Mrs Turner met us at the door to her classroom. 'Here,' she said, handing us a couple of blue marker pens. 'Write the verses with these. I will see you both at the next history lesson and let you know if you have done the work properly. I'm going off for my coffee break.'

While we were working, Charlotte glanced out of the classroom window into the playground beyond, where most of the pupils were hanging about in groups talking and eating crisps or chocolate bars.

'Hey, look who's out there,' she said excitedly. 'Isn't that the man from the Space Agency?'

I followed her gaze and watched as the man approached one group after another. He seemed to be checking what they were eating for break.

'Why's he interested in what everyone's eating or drinking?' Charlotte asked in a puzzled voice. We both stopped scribbling and watched as he went to the next group of children.

'He's not looking at what they've got *in* their hands,' I said suddenly. 'He's checking the hands themselves. Look, he's got Amanda Smith's hands under that magnifying glass.' I turned to Charlotte, as puzzled as she was. Then I glanced down at her hand, holding the marker pen.

'Blimey,' I exclaimed in dismay. 'Look at your fingers Charlotte! The tips are a flecked green colour!'

Charlotte looked down at her hands and gave a little squeal. 'What is it, Will?'

But I was too busy inspecting my own hands to worry about hers. Each of my fingertips had turned a pale mottled green, almost exactly the same colour as the slime I'd found on the edge of Dad's chisel; the chisel that had chipped away at the meteorite.

Contamination

6

'Do you think that's what he's checking everyone's hands for?' Charlotte asked, trying to rub the green stain off with a tissue. 'What is this stuff, Will? Do you think it's from the meteorite?'

'I don't know,' I said. 'But there was slime this colour on the edge of the chisel that Jun Mo was using to chip bits off the ice ball.'

'How does that man know about it though?' Charlotte asked, spitting on her fingers and rubbing them again. 'Ooh, I hope it isn't poisonous!'

Glancing out of the window again, I saw the man glance in our direction. I ducked back, flattening myself against the classroom wall, but when I looked again he was staring right at me.

'Oh, no, he's seen me,' I said. 'I hope that doesn't mean he's going to come indoors. He probably thought all the pupils were outside at playtime.' Grabbing up the marker pen I pulled the tissue out of Charlotte's hand and dragged her over to the white board. 'Quick, rub your fingers in this!'

Scribbling the pen onto one corner of the board,

we put our hands onto the wet ink and swirled them around until both of us had inky blue fingers, then I rubbed out the mess with the board rubber and stood back just as the door to the classroom opened behind us.

'Why aren't you children outside?' barked the man from the Space Agency.

Close up I could see that he was a strange looking man, tall and skinny, with a complexion that looked like he'd spent too long in a dark room and had grown all pasty and weedy.

But there was nothing weedy about his expression. 'Well?' he demanded.

'We're in detention, sir,' I said politely. No point in getting his back up by being cheeky, I thought.

'Show me your hands,' he said shortly.

'I thought you were from the Space Agency sir,' I said, pretending to be surprised by his request. 'Why do you want to see our hands?'

'We're doing a survey,' he said vaguely.

We both meekly held out our hands and the man leaned closer to inspect them.

'Filthy!' he said in disgust.

But it wasn't his displeasure that made me take a quick intake of breath and back away from him. His jacket had fallen open when he'd leaned forwards and there, in plain view, strapped against the side of his chest was a leather holster. And in it was the unmistakable grey metal outline of a gun.

I glanced at Charlotte and from her wide eyed look of shock I guessed she'd seen it too.

'Anyone else in detention?' he snapped, appearing not to notice our terrified expressions.

'I don't know sir,' I said faintly.

'Oh, never mind, I'll go and check for myself,' he said. And he turned on his heel and left the classroom.

'Jun Mo was right,' Charlotte breathed, holding on to a nearby desk for support as if her legs had almost given way under her. 'That man had a gun!'

'Jun Mo!' I said, suddenly remembering that he was in the next block doing his maths detention. 'We've got to warn him to disguise his hands before that weirdo sees them. He's bound to have got the green stuff on his hands too!'

Abandoning the history verses, we shot out into the corridor, determined to get to Jun Mo before the man did.

'He'll have gone that way,' I said, pointing to the obvious route down the hallway. 'Let's run up the stairs here and go through the geography classrooms; we might be able to get to the maths block first!'

We ran for the stairs, taking the steps two at a time, galloped through the empty geography classrooms and down the back stairs that led out into the playground. We were almost at the maths block when Charlotte tugged on the sleeve of my blazer, and we stopped dead, panting and gasping for air.

'That's him!' she cried. 'He must have simply glanced in to all the other classrooms on the way and come straight here. He's going to get to Jun Mo before we can warn him!'

We followed the man at a distance, nipping across the playground and ducking behind groups of pupils in case he looked back and saw us. Once inside the maths block we stopped at the door of each empty classroom until we were sure he hadn't seen us. When we got to the classroom where Jun Mo was working we flattened ourselves against the wall outside, trying to listen.

'My name is Mr Temoc,' we heard him say to Jun Mo. 'I have been invited here today by your headmaster and I am doing a survey on human hands. Please show me your hands, boy.'

Peeking through the gap in the door, I saw Jun Mo slowly hold out his hands. Charlotte closed her eyes and I felt a sinking feeling somewhere in my stomach. Mr Temoc or whatever his name was, would see the green stain and know we had found and touched a meteorite, and then the secret of our sudden cleverness would be out. Not only that, but the Space Agency would probably come snooping round to my house and then Mum and Dad would want to know why I hadn't told them a meteorite had landed on our shed. A part of me asked if it mattered one jot who knew about it, but another part of me wanted to keep our secret safe, just for a while longer. And anyway, I thought defiantly, what was so important about that meteorite? What was urgent enough for an armed man to come sneaking round our school interrogating people?

'He's coming out!' hissed Charlotte, bringing me quickly back to our present dilemma. 'Run!'

We sped to the next classroom along the corridor and dived inside, nearly colliding with each other in the doorway in our haste. Hiding behind the door, we listened to his footsteps as they receded down the corridor. Jun Mo didn't seem to be with him. After a few minutes we peered out again; the man was gone.

'Come on,' I said, dragging Charlotte behind me by her blue hands. We looked into the maths classroom to find Jun Mo poring over his maths sheet. He looked up when we panted in.

'You finished your detention already?' he asked, obviously surprised to see us.

'We didn't do it,' Charlotte told him, 'well only a bit of it. That man…Mr Temoc, he's been checking everyone's hands! Let's see your hands, Jun Mo.'

Jun Mo held out his hands. 'What's everyone want to see my hands for?' he asked, obviously puzzled by the request.

We both stared at Jun Mo's hands in surprise. His fingers were as short and stubby as ever, but they were clean; not a hint of green about them.

'Oh,' I said, a little disappointed. 'Well maybe what's happened to ours has nothing to do with the meteorite after all.'

At that moment the bell rang for the end of break time, and Jun Mo picked up his completed paper and put it on the teacher's desk.

'Someone better tell me what's going on,' he said as we hurried out into the corridor again.

We filled him in on what little we knew on our way to the science lab and showed him our newly inked hands. 'Our finger tips are green under here,' I whispered as a couple of people pushed past us. 'Both of us; it's a bit odd isn't it?'

'And you saw a gun?' Jun Mo said, his eyes gleaming excitedly. 'I told you he had a gun.'

'Never mind the gun,' Charlotte said, 'I want to know why we're turning green and you're not.'

'You touched the space ice,' Jun Mo said simply.

'So did you!' Charlotte exclaimed.

'No,' Jun Mo said as we took our seats at the back of the lab. 'I touched the chisel and hammer. You put the ice in the bag with your hands.'

We were just digesting this piece of information when the door to the lab opened and Mr Temoc appeared. Both Charlotte and I slid our hands under the work bench out of sight.

'I am Mr Temoc, from the Space Agency,' he began. 'Your science teacher has asked me to take his class today.' His beady eyes stared round the room. 'So I will tell you a little about meteorites, if you would all sit still and shut up.'

The class instantly fell silent, unused to being spoken to like that. A boy at the front giggled and Mr Temoc turned his cold eyes on him.

'You, boy, tell me what you know about meteorites.'

'They er… come from space sir.'

'They do indeed,' Mr Temoc said. 'Small fragments of rocky or metallic space debris – called meteoroids, sometimes enter the Earth's atmosphere where they usually burn up. The result is a bright streak in the sky, known as a meteor or shooting star. Dust trails from comets cause regular meteor showers, like the ones we have seen on the news over the last few nights. 'Meteorites' are what we call the ones that actually collide with the Earth.'

He paused and stared round at the silent class. 'Any questions so far?'

'What's the difference between a comet and a meteor sir?' asked the boy in the front.

'Comets are like large dirty snowballs,' Mr Temoc said.

Jun Mo, Charlotte and I all snapped to attention. Was it a comet that had crashed through the shed roof then?

'They originate in distant regions of the Solar System beyond Pluto,' he continued. 'Sometimes the gravity of a passing star pushes a comet into the inner Solar System where it orbits the sun. Occasionally a comet is visible from Earth.'

The boy in the front put his hand up. None of us much liked Simon Clarke, but we were glad he was asking the questions this time.

'Yes, boy?'

'Can comets crash to earth sir?'

'If you'd bothered to listen you stupid boy, you'd know you have heard the answer already,' said Mr Temoc sourly. 'When a comet passes near to the sun its crust begins to melt and the dust and gases make a trail – called the coma.' He stared belligerently at the class. 'Who remembers what I told you all of five seconds ago?'

Amanda Smith put her hand up tentatively. 'Trails from comets make regular meteor showers, sir.'

'Ah, the girl with green felt tip pen all over her hands,' Mr Temoc said. 'Glad you're not wasting my time again. Yes, the *trail* of comets can cause meteor showers. Does that sound to you like the whole flaming comet comes crashing to Earth?' He stared round the room again and people wriggled uncomfortably in their seats. 'Now I have a question for you lot. Have any of you seen anything unusual in the sky recently?'

We all sat as still as possible, avoiding the man's searching eyes. He sighed audibly and rolled his eyes as if he thought we were all the most stupid creatures he'd ever had the misfortune to talk to. After a few minutes of total silence, he said, 'Right, you can all clear off then. Get lost, the lot of you.'

And he stomped off out of the science lab and into the next classroom, presumably to give his enjoyable talk all over again.

Sports Day

7

I have to admit that even after the worryingly eventful morning, the sports day went rather well for Jun Mo, Charlotte and me. Jun Mo won the field events, javelin and shot put by miles, getting two gold medals. Charlotte, who always did well with the running races anyway, came first in the 200, 500 and 800 metre races, winning three more golds and I jumped by far the highest and furthest in high jump and long jump, for two more gold medals.

We were all entered into the cross country, which I usually came fourth or fifth in, Charlotte was usually close by, and Jun Mo normally trailed in somewhere near the back. Today, however, we came in first, second and third and went away with more medals hanging round our necks. I was glad that the creepy Mr Temoc had decided not to stay to watch the events as our successes might very well have given us away.

As the results were announced, our friends became more and more grumpy, until there were noticeably more groans going up than the cheering we were expecting.

'I don't think we're very popular,' I whispered to Charlotte as we walked back across the field to get changed to go home. 'And I was so looking forward to showing everyone what I could do.'

'No one likes a smart Alec,' she said with more brightness than I felt. 'Anyway, this new being clever at everything will probably soon wear off now the meteorite's gone, and we'll be back to our old selves.'

The thought was sobering. Despite the fact that our new found skills had caused us nothing but trouble, I quite liked being top of something for a change. It felt good; I felt like king of the world.

The sense of euphoria soon wore off when I got home. Luke was waiting just inside the front door with his normal greeting, 'Hi squib. How did it go at school today?'

Unable to resist showing off, I showed him my collection of medals.

'Blimey, mate, where did you steal those from?'

'I won them,' I said proudly.

'You! Win something…give me a break.'

And he punched me hard on the arm.

'Don't,' I said, rubbing my arm. 'Or you'll be sorry.'

Grabbing me roughly he wrestled me to the ground, pinning me in a head lock. 'Who thinks he's a clever little Billy then?' he taunted.

He twisted hard at the medals hanging round my neck until my eyes began to water.

'Stop it, Luke, I mean it!' I croaked as he continued to choke me.

'Promise you'll give me your new CD collection and I'll let you go,' he said jovially. 'Promise you'll give your big brother exactly what he wants.'

'I promise to give you exactly what you deserve,' I snarled. And in one swift movement I crushed his hand away from my throat, twisted his arm behind his back and tipped my weight round so that he was face down on the floor and I was on top of him, squashing his face into the carpet.

'You're not having my CD's,' I said quietly from my position of power. Get your own.' And I let go of him and stood up.

Luke lay there for a moment, too shocked to move. Then he got slowly to his feet and brushed himself down. 'I didn't want your CD's anyway,' he said in a hurt voice. 'I was only playing.'

'Yeah, so was I,' I said, my face breaking into a grin. 'Let me know when you want to play again.'

There were only two more days until the end of term, and Jun Mo, Charlotte and I spent most of them getting into trouble. Even though we'd decided to do our best NOT to come top of everything, we found it nearly impossible.

'It's so difficult trying to remember how much of a subject I'm supposed to know when I look at it and understand everything so clearly,' she complained as we sat in yet another detention for cheating, this time an after school one. 'I mean, that essay I wrote for Miss Hill just came to me. All I did was write what she asked and she seemed to think I'd got a dictionary or some sort of mini laptop hidden somewhere about my person. It's just not fair.'

'I think I might be a nuclear physicist,' Jun Mo announced dreamily, 'Physics is so easy now.'

'Yeah, I was thinking of doing medicine,' I said. 'I've always wanted to be a vet, but my grades weren't up to it before.'

'It's no good being clever if the teachers won't believe it's our own work,' Charlotte grumbled, staring out at the fine summer rain that was beating against the classroom window. 'And it certainly isn't making us popular in class.'

Jun Mo laughed, 'My parents are pleased with my medals though! I got a double helping of dinner after sports day.'

'At least Mr Creepy Temoc hasn't been back again,' Charlotte said with a shiver. 'My fingers are as green as ever.'

'At least it hasn't spread,' I said. 'I was worried it might go on up my arms and then into my body and turn me into an alien.'

Charlotte turned to me with a look of horror on her face. 'You don't think that's why we're so changed?' she said. 'You don't think drinking that space ice has made us into something sub human, like in that film where everyone turns into zombies?'

Jun Mo stood up and held his arms out in front of him, shuffling towards Charlotte with a vacant look on his face until she screeched for him to stop it.

'Look, I'm being serious!' she said. 'There has to be a reason why the Space Agency sent that man to our school. And he was definitely looking for people with green hands, you heard what he said to Amanda Smith in the science lab about not wasting his time again…as if she had wasted his time already when he spotted her with green felt tip pen on her hands and he thought it was something else.'

'And there's another thing,' I put in suddenly. 'Do you remember what Temoc said to Jun Mo when he was checking his hands in the maths room and we were hiding outside the door? He said he was doing a survey on *human* hands…don't you think that was a very strange thing to say?'

'Looking at Jun Mo now, I think it was perfectly reasonable,' Charlotte said as Jun Mo lurched zombie-like towards her. 'I'm just surprised he passed the test!'

'I think I'll go and have another look at the crater in the shed floor when I get home,' I said glancing at my watch. 'I know it looked like the ice thing had melted completely when we went back to look on Sunday, but maybe there is some clue left in the dust and rocks as to what the Space Agency are interested in, that we missed.'

Eventually we were allowed to leave, with a strict warning from the deputy head that cheating was not going to be tolerated next term.

'There is only one morning of school left this term,' he reminded us unnecessarily. 'So let's not have any more of this silliness. Whatever it is you're doing, it has to stop.'

'Yes sir,' we chorused meekly, whilst giving each

other knowing looks from under our lashes.

'Off you go now,' he said, a little more kindly. 'Get yourselves off home.'

The first thing I did when I got home was to check that Luke wasn't back from college yet. Dad wasn't home either, but Mum was in the kitchen making dinner. I called hello as I shrugged out of my blazer, wrenched off my school tie and headed out of the back door.

It had stopped raining a few minutes before, but the grass was still very wet, so I stuck to the path and arrived at the shed door a moment later. Putting out my hand, I slowly pushed the door open, and peered inside. What I saw nearly took my breath away.

'Crikey! Bloody 'ell,' I said loudly, taking a step backwards.

I stood for a moment trying to collect my thoughts while drips of water plopped from the shed roof and ran down the neck of my school shirt. The wet grass smell of the newly rained on garden filled my nostrils, but it was still muggy and warm, and a faint sweat had broken out over my whole body.

Taking a tentative step forwards again, I peered back into the shed, my eyes wide with disbelief. Through the gaping hole on the far side of the roof, a thin beam of watery sunshine filtered down onto a tropical paradise; thick green ferns uncurling towards the light, a bright moss covered floor, a brown pool of water filling the crater below.

Slowly, careful not to tread on any of the newly

sprouting plants, I inched towards the crater. A creeper vine of some sort swung nearby and I pushed it out of the way for a better view. There, partly visible above the dirty water something was shining palely.

Reaching out a green finger tip towards the thing, I held my breath. Should I touch it I thought? Was it safe? What could it be?

Rocking back on my haunches, I contemplated the object for a few minutes, while new vines and ferns twitched and stretched towards the ray of sunlight. It felt like the whole interior of the shed had come alive with the rain and was vibrating and trembling with new life.

Pulling back my hand and getting to my feet, I turned and left the shed, clicking the door closed behind me. Out in the still garden I drew in a great gasping breath of fresh air and then started to run towards the house.

'Mum!' I yelled as I shot in through the back door. 'Can I invite Charlotte and Jun Mo round this evening?'

'I suppose so,' she said. 'But what's all the rush? You break up tomorrow and then you've got the whole of the summer holidays to see them.'

'I'd really like them to come over now,' I wheedled. 'Please, Mum?'

'Go on then,' she said, turning back to her cooking. 'I'll put some extra pasta on for them.'

'Thanks Mum,' I said, giving her an unaccustomed hug. 'You're the best.'

I could hardly press the dials on my mobile 'phone, my hands were shaking so hard. When Jun Mo answered, my voice came out in a strangled gasp, 'Jun Mo, you've got to come and see this! It's the shed…it's like a tropical jungle, there's plants and everything, and the crater has filled with rain water.'

'You're joking!'

'No, honestly, Jun Mo, and there's something in the crater too, only I'm not sure what it is…you've got to come!'

'Okay, I'll ask my parents,' he said. And the line went dead.

Pressing the keys for Charlotte's number, I told her the same thing, 'You have to come over,' I begged her. 'There's something weird in the crater.'

'Mum's just called me for tea,' she said. 'Can I come later?'

'My mum will get you some tea,' I said. I was getting frustrated by her inability to realise how amazing this thing was. 'Please come as soon as you can!'

'What sort of thing is it in the crater?' she asked. 'Is it a piece of the meteorite?'

Lowering my voice to a whisper, I cupped the 'phone to my face with my hand. 'Charlotte,' I hissed, 'I think it might be something alive…a creature of some sort.'

'What do you mean alive?'

'Come and see for yourself. I think I might have discovered an alien life form.'

Alien

8

Three quarters of an hour later we were sitting round the kitchen table trying not to meet one another's eyes. Having summoned Jun Mo and Charlotte here in huge excitement I had to be patient as Mum had insisted we sat and ate dinner before we 'disappeared off somewhere' as she put it. Luke and Dad who were both home by this time kept glancing from one of us to the other as if they suspected we were up to something.

When we'd finished the meal I was heartily relieved to hear Luke ask Dad for a lift to his friend's house. At least he wouldn't be hanging around trying to find out what we were up to, I thought. Luke had been treating me with a bit more respect since yesterday, I noticed, but that didn't mean he'd leave us in peace.

Jun Mo, Charlotte and I were just heading for the back door, when Dad called to me, 'William! Have you done your homework?'

'Dad, we're breaking up at lunchtime tomorrow, we haven't got any.' I said.

'Okay, if you're sure. See you later.'

Is it possible to hurry slowly? If it is, then that is what we did on the way to the shed. Our excitement was mingled with apprehension. What would we find when we opened the shed door? Would the thing still be there…if it was anything at all and not some paper bag that had blown in through the jagged roof hole?

Standing outside the shed, I felt almost sick. I wished I hadn't eaten quite so much of Mum's pasta. My stomach seemed to be doing little loop the loops in my belly.

Glancing at the other two, I noticed that they had gone very quiet. I believe the saying 'take the bull by the horns' means that if you are committed to do something you may as well get on with it, and give it your best shot. So I grabbed the proverbial bull's horns and yanked open the shed door, so that it swung right back on its hinges with a bang.

We all stared speechlessly into the wondrous interior. The ferns and climbers had grown even more in the last couple of hours so they were almost touching the shed's ceiling.

'Crikey!' said Jun Mo in a reasonable Aussie accent, considering he was Korean.

'It's unbelievable!' breathed Charlotte, peering over my shoulder. 'There was nothing here two days ago.'

'Except space ice,' Jun Mo said, stepping over the threshold and looking round with shining eyes. 'Wow…this is like a jungle.'

We all clambered inside, stepping over slimy

stems and great shiny looking green leaves. The evening sun was filtering down from the hole between the ferns causing a speckled effect which made it hard to see.

'Where's the crater?' Jun Mo whispered.

'Over there.'

'How did it get full of water?' Charlotte asked.

'From today's rain, I expect,' I said vaguely. I was hardly listening to them, because I had spotted the pale shiny thing floating in the water and was trying to make out what it was.

Slowly, I crouched down next to the crater and reached out a hand.

'Don't touch it!' Charlotte squealed. 'We don't know what it is, it might be dangerous.'

She turned and went out of the shed, returning in a few moments with a broken piece of cane from Mum's runner bean plants.

'Here, poke it with this,' she said.

Taking the cane from her, I gave the thing a gentle poke, but the cane went straight through as if there was nothing there.

'Do it again,' Jun Mo encouraged.

This time I poked harder and although I still couldn't feel anything under the cane, to our astonishment the thing turned in the water, rolling and swirling like a thin wispy vapour. Gradually the misty substance took on the shape of a body and head, its long thin arms wrapped round its knees. We stared in wide eyed wonder as the thing opened one wrinkled eyelid and peered up at me.

'It's a baby!' cried Charlotte in astonishment.

'Funny looking baby,' commented Jun Mo.

Slowly the funny looking baby unwound one of its long arms and reached out towards me. I felt like the boy in ET when the alien touched him with his abnormally long finger. But there was no glowing light on the end of this creature's finger. Its finger tip was green, just like mine.

'What's it made from?' Charlotte asked, leaning closer to inspect the creature as it lay floating in the puddle formed by the meteorite crater. 'It looks sort of transparent.'

'That's why it looked shiny, I suppose,' I said, gazing into the creature's one open eye. 'It's reflecting the sunshine, look here, where the sun's ray touches it. It looks like soft reflective glass.'

'It wants to touch you,' Jun Mo said.

'Do you think you should?' Charlotte warned.

'Probably not,' I said as I reached out and rested one green finger against the creature's outstretched digit.

'What does it feel like?' Charlotte asked softly

'Ice cold,' I said immediately. 'It's not a mammal, that's for sure.'

'It's moving,' said Jun Mo. And sure enough the creature was wriggling and writhing suddenly in the water; its finger still touching mine as it splashed and gurgled.

'Look at its face,' said Charlotte. 'It's taking on human features.'

We all watched, entranced as the thing continued

to thrash about. It appeared to be growing bigger by the second. And then it stopped and lay still, its body so big now that the water was hardly visible beneath it. It turned intelligent eyes on us and Charlotte gave a loud squeal. 'Oh, I don't believe it! It looks just like you, Will.'

The creature removed its finger from mine and sat up; blinking and staring round at the interior of the shed, then it focused his eyes on us. It seemed to stare at me with a horrified expression on its face. *My face* I realised with a jolt of fear.

Jun Mo started to laugh.

'What's so funny?' I demanded huffily.

'It looks the same,' he giggled.

'Its expression is mirroring yours, Will,' Charlotte explained. 'Don't look so scared. Try smiling.'

Stretching my face into the semblance of a grin, I watched mesmerised as the creature's expression changed to a twisted smile.

Jun Mo fell about laughing. 'Try this,' he said, pushing his finger against his nose and flattening it so he looked like a pig.

I copied Jun Mo and watched in wonder as the creature reached out a long pale hand and squashed its own nose up against its face.

'Can you speak?' I asked the creature.

We watched as its mouth moved silently, mirroring mine, but no words came out.

For the next few minutes we put the creature through its paces, testing his ability to copy me in a variety of poses. At last we fell silent, realising for the first time that we actually had quite a problem on our hands.

'Do you think it can walk?' Charlotte asked at length.

I got to my feet and took a few steps between the crowded plants. The creature unfolded its spindly limbs and stood. Then it walked a few paces and sat down opposite me.

'Looks like it can,' I said, 'What are we going to do with it?'

'Pity it's the end of term,' Jun Mo commented, 'You could have bunked off lessons, leaving this thing in your place.'

'Yeah,' I smiled at Jun Mo's idea. The creature smiled in exactly the same way and my smile vanished. So did the creatures.

'This could get tiresome,' I said.

'We can't keep referring to it as a thing,' Charlotte said. 'We ought to give him a name; and some clothes.'

'Will Two,' said Jun Mo.

'No way! How about 'Ice Man'?' I suggested. 'He's cold enough.'

'He's more of a boy than a man,' Charlotte pointed out. 'Why don't we just call him Ice?'

'Yeah, Ice,' said Jun Mo.

Leaning towards my mirror image, I mouthed the word Ice at him and pointed to his chest.

The creature opened his mouth, copying mine, but no sound came out.

'Give him your shirt or something,' Charlotte said suddenly. 'It's really odd sitting here with a naked version of you, Will.'

I hurriedly pulled off my white school shirt and handed it to Ice. He just sat and stared at it.

'Mime putting it on and see if he'll copy you,' said Charlotte.

'Here, like this,' I said, putting my arms back into the shirt sleeves. I took it off again and handed it back to Ice.

Slowly, he reached out a hand and took the shirt from me, pushing one hand through an armhole and then the other.

And then something really peculiar happened; Ice vanished.

One minute he was pulling the shirt on and the next, all we could see was the grubby white of the cotton shirt. It seemed to hang in mid air as if suspended on an invisible coat hanger.

'Where's he gone?' Charlotte exclaimed, and she leaned forwards and put her arms round the hovering shirt. 'I can feel him!' she cried, 'he's still here, but now he's mirroring the shirt!'

'Does he still feel human?' I asked, reaching across to touch the shirt with Ice presumably somewhere within it.

'I don't know exactly,' Charlotte replied. 'Wait, yes, I can feel his presence.'

'What's it doing now?' Jun Mo shouted suddenly, for the shirt was leaping about as if it was a thing possessed. Then, as we watched, the creature changed gradually back to human shape and form. Only this time it looked like a female.

'It's Charlotte,' Jun Mo said breathlessly.

I peered closely at the human figure which had materialised before me holding Charlotte's hand. It had long blonde hair and the most beautiful eyes: Charlotte's blue green eyes with their amazing brown flecks. Fortunately for Charlotte this female Ice was now wearing the school shirt he had been only a moment ago, which although unbuttoned, managed to cover her to the top of her thighs.

Charlotte shook the thing's hand loose from her grasp and quickly buttoned the shirt up to its neck for it.

'There, that's better,' she said, with a pink flush to her cheeks. 'I'm not sure how accurate that thing can be when it copies us but I think I'd rather it stayed dressed.'

Ice stood and stared at Charlotte with interest. I realised that that was how Charlotte was looking at it.

And then suddenly we all froze; for Mum was calling us, and from the sound of her voice, she was on her way down the garden to find us.

The Project

9

We managed to tumble out of the shed just before Mum reached us, and we stood guiltily in a row with our backs pressed against the shed door.

'What are you up to?' she said suspiciously. 'I've been calling you for ages. Charlotte's mother has been on the 'phone asking what time she wants collecting.'

'We're doing a project,' Charlotte said hastily.

'What sort of project? It's nearly the end of term.'

'Er...a gardening project. We've got to make a tropical environment in our back gardens over the summer holidays,' Charlotte lied inventively.

'Oh yes?' said Mum. 'Well don't expect much help from Will. He hates gardening, don't you Will?'

'I think it might be a challenge,' I said, 'And I enjoy a challenge.'

Mum's eyes narrowed, but she just nodded. 'So what time shall I tell her? Don't forget you've all still got to get up in the morning for your last half day at school.'

'Will nine o'clock be alright?' Charlotte asked.

'Yes, that's fine. I'm glad you're all out here getting some fresh air instead of being cooped up indoors watching DVD's. It's turned lovely now the rain has stopped again.'

And she turned on her heel and returned to the house where she was probably in the middle of a work out.

'Phew!' I said as she disappeared from sight. 'That was close. Well done for your quick thinking, Charlotte. Now if anyone does go into the shed for any reason, they will just think this is all part of our project.'

'It's very bad to lie to your parents,' Jun Mo said disapprovingly, glaring at us.

'I'm sorry Jun Mo,' she said, 'but we could hardly say we were hiding an alien in there could we?'

One by one we filed back into the shed, expecting to see the Ice Charlotte still waiting for us, but instead he or she seemed to have vanished. My shirt was lying on the shed floor, but when we felt it we realised it was empty of any life forms.

'Where's he gone?' asked Jun Mo looking round.

We searched the shed from end to end but with no luck. Ice had somehow disappeared completely. We searched for him for another twenty minutes, but then gave up and trooped back to the house.

Mum was sitting at the table poring over a document of some sort, but she got up when we came in and asked if we wanted cold drinks. I realised I was really thirsty, it had been warm and damp in the shed just like a real tropical rainforest was supposed to be.

As we sat sipping at our drinks I glanced at the form Mum had been filling in.

'What's that?'

'Some sort of survey from the Space Agency,' Mum replied. 'They want to know if we've seen anything of that meteor shower that's been on the news recently.'

I looked more closely at the form. It asked the householder to fill in the details of what they'd seen or heard and on which night.

'What have you put down?' I asked, trying to sound casual.

'That we haven't seen or heard anything,' Mum said. 'Although it does ask if we were actually home or not for each date. I suppose I'd better put that we were out on Saturday night.'

'But we were here, Mrs Alexander,' said Charlotte. 'That would count wouldn't it?'

'Well, yes, I suppose it would,' Mum said and she put a tick in the box which asked if anyone was home on Saturday night and a cross in the box which asked if anyone had seen anything unusual, then she folded the form and put it in its reply paid envelope.

'I wonder how many people are taking part in the survey,' I said. 'Do you think it's the whole country?'

'I think it's just this area,' Mum said. 'I believe there was supposed to be a lot of meteor activity in the skies about here, though I haven't seen anything myself. I expect it's been too cloudy, that's what usually happens when there's anything exciting to look at.'

At nine o'clock Charlotte's parents came for her and they offered to give Jun Mo a lift home too. I decided to have one last peek into the shed before coming indoors to watch TV.

Despite the fact that it was still light in the garden, the inside of the shed was gloomy. So many plants had sprouted from the earth floor and shot up to the ceiling, they were almost blocking the hole in the roof where the late evening sunlight was trying to get in. I searched one more time for Ice, even swishing at the dirty water in the crater in case he'd somehow shrunk down and gone back to where we first found him, but I had no luck.

I was just about to leave the shed and return to the house, when one of the big shiny leaved plants brushed against me, making me jump. The plant leaned towards me as if it were being blown by a stiff wind, but there was no feeling of a draught coming into the shed. I stared at the plant with interest and it curled its topmost tip down until it was almost touching my face. If a plant could look interested, then this one certainly did.

'Ice?' I asked hesitantly. 'Is that you?'

Holding out a green tipped finger, I touched one of the pointy bits on the side of a particularly large leaf. Almost immediately the plant began to shake. I watched fascinated as it began to take on human shape and form and then suddenly I was looking into a face that I recognised very well; the one I saw reflected in the bathroom mirror every morning.

'Crikey, mate,' I said with a grin. 'You know how

to give a fellow a nasty turn don't you?'

Ice grinned back and I was gripped by the wish that he could talk. Taking one of his ice cold hands, I guided his freezing fingers towards my throat, to where I imagined my vocal cords might lie. 'Here, copy here,' I told him, and I pressed his fingers against my voice box while I made a series of words and sounds, watching his throat all the time for any sign that he was duplicating my voice box.

'Now say, 'hello, hell…o,' I instructed. 'Go on Ice, try it.'

Ice formed his mouth into an E shape followed by an O, but no sound came out of his mouth.

'Oh, well,' I told him. 'Never mind.' Glancing at my watch, I prised his icy fingers away from my neck which felt like it was getting frost bite and backed towards the door. 'I have to go. It'll be dark soon. I'll come and see you tomorrow afternoon when school finishes.'

And I started to leave the shed. Only Ice seemed to think he was coming too.

'Hey, you can't come out!' I said, pushing him back inside. 'You'll get lost out here. It's nearly dark, and anyway, you haven't got any clothes on.'

He let me push him back alright, but as soon as I turned to leave again, he was beside me, trying to get out of the door alongside me.

'No,' I said firmly, pushing him back again. 'You have to stay here.'

I tried to leave three times and each time Ice tried to come with me. In the end I stood scratching my head, wondering what to do. Ice stood and scratched his head too.

'Okay,' I said at last. 'I've got an idea.' Reaching round Ice, I pulled one of the trailing vines towards him and started to wrap it round his body. Almost immediately Ice began to take on the shape and colour of the vine and better still, he was attached to the floor of the shed by a series of long tapering roots.

'See you tomorrow,' I called as I closed the shed door on the thicket of vines and creepers.

'Who are you talking to?' asked a voice. I realised with a start that someone was standing in the shadows by one of the apple trees in the garden. I recognised the voice with a sinking feeling in my stomach; it was Luke.

'No one,' I said.

'Well now little bro', either you're lying to your big brother, or you're going off your trolley.'

'I thought you went out,' I said warily.

'I did. Then I came back.'

'It's getting dark out here,' I said, trying to take his mind off the fact he'd heard me talking to someone he couldn't see.'

'So what are you doing out here all on your lonesome?' he persisted.

'I came to make sure the shed door was closed,' I replied. 'Jun Mo, Charlotte and I are doing a project in there.'

'What zort of project?' he said, slurring his words slightly.

'Gardening,' I told him, deciding to stick with Charlotte's invention. 'We're making a tropical rainforest.' I peered at him closely. 'Have you been drinking?'

'I might have had a few beers,' he said, instantly on his guard. 'What's it to you?'

'Nothing, only its easy to imagine you've seen or heard things that aren't real if you're half drunk.'

Luke scowled at me. 'You'd better not say anything to Mum or Dad,' he warned me. 'And anyway I'm not drunk. It takes more than a couple of beers to get me drunk, little bro'.'

'So why did you say you thought you heard me talking to someone?' I persisted. 'When there's no one here?'

He swayed on his feet and thought about this for a few minutes and I almost laughed. Luke thought it was so clever to have a few drinks, when the very fact he'd been drinking made it so easy to get one over on him. It was like playing with a rather stupid child, when in fact Luke was pretty smart when he was sober.

Luke obviously felt that somehow I'd made a fool of him and he lurched towards me with his hands clenched into fists. I waited while he came at me then stepped to one side at the last minute and he went sprawling head first into the shed wall.

'Ow!' he said, holding his head whilst trying to scramble awkwardly to his feet, 'I'll get you for that.'

'Oh yeah?'

'Yeah!'

And he charged me again, rather like an ungainly teenage bull, his head down and his muscles tensed, intent on a fight. Hoping my new found powers were still with me, I stood my ground until he was almost upon me, then made a fist with my hand and held it in front of me. Luke ran straight into it and fell to the ground, groaning.

'You little runt...I'll get you for that!' he said again. But this time he didn't get to his feet but just lay there, watching me warily.

'I don't want to fight you,' I said, staring down at him, and to my surprise, he grinned suddenly and clambered to his feet.

'Let's be friends then,' he said amiably. Luke was like that; he could change from one mood to another in an instant. I thought to myself as we walked back to the house together with one of Luke's arms draped loosely over my shoulders that he wasn't unlike Ice in some ways because you never quite knew what you were going to get. And just like with Ice, I'd been able to turn Luke's supposed talents against him.

I laughed as I climbed into bed later that night, picturing Luke running headlong into my fist and then chuckled some more when I pictured Ice, trapped in the shed by his own copy-cat ability to take on the likeness of a plant that was anchored to the floor by its roots.

The Fight

10

The last morning of the term turned out to be a disaster. Charlotte and I had both been told off repeatedly for having green paint on our hands. I had been sent off to the washrooms several times, but of course the stuff wouldn't wash off; it was part of our fingers.

Charlotte was more worried about it that me. Apparently her mother had tried to get it off her the night before, using white spirit and then some industrial strength cleaner that was supposed to remove virtually any stain. Charlotte was convinced she was going to have to stay green forever and was close to tears.

At break time I told Jun Mo and Charlotte about what had happened with Ice and Luke, and Jun Mo thought it was brilliant. Charlotte clapped her hands to her mouth and asked fearfully what would happen if Ice did leave the shed.

'Well, the fact that when he takes human form he's naked is a problem,' I admitted. 'Worse if he happens to look like me at the time. I mean, I don't want people to think I've taken to walking round the

71

neighbourhood in nothing but my birthday suit.'

'What if he looks like me?' Charlotte shrieked. 'Suppose he goes wandering about looking like me with nothing on? Oh my God, I'd never live it down. If someone saw me naked I'd have to emigrate to Australia or something.'

'I'd emigrate to ruddy Australia if I saw you naked,' laughed a voice behind us.

We were standing in a corner of the playground where we thought we could talk without being overheard, but we turned to find a group of the year's thugs staring at us. Gavin, the biggest of the three, was gaping at Charlotte with a sort of disgusted leer on his face, and Charlotte had turned a bright shade of crimson at his insult.

'You take that back,' I said coldly.

'You gonna make me?' Gavin sneered.

'I'll make you,' Jun Mo said, stepping between Charlotte and the thug.

'Oh, leave him alone Jun Mo,' Charlotte said shakily. 'He's not worth it.'

Before I could utter another word, Gavin had given Jun Mo a push that should have sent him reeling, but which actually just rocked him back slightly on his heels.

Gavin looked at Jun Mo in surprise. He'd obviously expected Jun Mo to fall over. The other two thugs, Malcolm and Wayne stepped forwards to back up their leader and Charlotte moved behind me at the sight of the grinning threesome who were plainly spoiling for a fight.

'Look, this is stupid,' I said, hoping to talk some sense into them. 'We'll all get into trouble if we start fighting in the playground.'

'You scared then?' Gavin taunted me. 'Wetting your pants with terror are you?'

'We'll get suspended if we don't all calm down,' I said, trying not to let his jibes rile me.

Gavin stepped as close as he could, almost pushing his ugly face into mine. 'Hit me, go on Alexander, hit me and see what happens.'

'I know what will happen,' I said calmly. 'I'll flatten you and then Jun Mo and I will flatten your gormless friends. It will be so easy that I really can't be bothered to do it.'

Gavin's face contorted with anger and his fist came up, ready to throw the first punch; but I was used to Luke using me as a punch bag and I ducked sideways as his fist sailed through the air, missing me by miles but almost landing in Charlotte's face.

Jun Mo gave a roar of anger and surged forwards, knocking Gavin off his feet. Jun Mo might be short in stature, but he was solid as a rock and with his new found powers he was virtually unstoppable. Malcolm and Wayne leapt to their friend's defence, but found themselves being bodily lifted off their feet and chucked sideways onto a patch of scrubby grass at the edge of the playground.

'Jun Mo, no!' shrieked Charlotte as he turned back to Gavin with his fists raised.

Gavin tried to scramble up, but I put a restraining foot on his chest, pinning him to the ground.

'Enough!' I said.

At that moment Mr Jarvis, the head of year rounded the corner of the building and hurried over to where the three boys were sprawled on the ground and Jun Mo was bent over them with his fist still raised in the air.

'What the devil's going on here?' he demanded.

'They attacked us, sir!' Gavin complained. 'We didn't do nothing sir, and they just went for us.'

'Is this true?' he asked the other two boys.

'Yes,' they both nodded. 'They're mental, them three.'

The head of year stared at Jun Mo, who had lowered his fist but was still red in the face with anger. 'Did you do this?'

'Yes,' Jun Mo said shortly, 'They're a bad lot.'

'Go to my office Jun Mo – right now!' the head of year instructed. 'The rest of you, go to your form rooms and stay there until I have got to the bottom of what happened here.'

'But it wasn't Jun Mo's fault…' Charlotte started.

Mr Jarvis held up his finger for silence. 'I will deal with each of you later. You will all have your turn to tell me exactly what happened.'

'But sir…'

'Later,' he said.

We missed the school play which usually took place instead of lessons on the last morning of the school year. The teachers took turns with the pupils to do a sketch and it was normally incredibly funny. I sat with Charlotte in our tutor classroom waiting to be summoned to Mr Jarvis's office. We could hear the distant laughter coming from the main hall and stared at one another miserably.

'Nothing's gone right since Ice appeared on the scene,' Charlotte complained, rubbing at her fingers with a tissue. 'I wish we'd never seen that rubbish meteorite.'

'We didn't really have much choice,' I reminded her. 'We'd have had to be either very deaf or else stupid to have missed a thing like that crashing through the roof.'

At that moment Mr Jarvis appeared in the doorway and strode over to us, his expression grave.

'I have spoken to Jun Mo and to the other three boys involved,' he said. 'It sounds as if there was some provocation by Gavin, Malcolm and Wayne. I am told that neither of you were actually involved in the fight. Do either of you have anything to say?'

'It wasn't exactly a fight sir,' I said hastily. 'And Jun Mo was only trying to protect Charlotte; we both were.'

'Look,' said Mr Jarvis taking on a more reasonable tone, 'I know the three of you aren't normally trouble makers, but you have been acting very strangely for the last couple of days. I don't know what's going on, but I don't want it to continue into next term, do I make myself clear?'

'Yes sir,' I said.

'What will happen to Jun Mo?' Charlotte asked, having given up trying to scrub off the green stain and hiding her hands behind her back.

'Well, apparently no punches were actually exchanged, so he will not be suspended. We will, however be writing a letter to his parents to tell them of his recent behaviour.'

'But sir,' I said. 'He only pushed them to stop them from hurting Charlotte!'

'He was really brave,' Charlotte added.

'The other boys have admitted that only pushing and shoving was involved,' Mr Jarvis said, nodding. 'But Malcolm has a nasty grass burn down one arm and Gavin has a twisted ankle where he fell awkwardly. Your friend must have given them the mightiest of pushes. Because of their injuries, we have to inform Jun Mo's parents.'

When the bell went for the end of school, we hurried off to find Jun Mo, who was emptying the contents of his locker into a kit bag.

'I'm so sorry you got into trouble,' Charlotte said, putting her arm round him. 'Thanks for sticking up for me.'

I could hardly look my friend in the eye. I had antagonised Gavin into trying to punch me and Jun Mo had got the blame. I felt pretty bad about it and wouldn't have been surprised if he wasn't speaking to me. Charlotte and I emptied our own lockers without saying anything else. When we'd got all our possessions stowed away, I turned to face him.

'Sorry Jun Mo,' I said. 'I should have taken more of the blame.'

'I'm sorry too,' he said. 'I should have punched them all real quick, before the teacher came.'

'Then you'd have been suspended or even expelled,' Charlotte exclaimed. 'Honestly, you boys!'

We all laughed and the tension between us was broken.

'Do you want to come back to my place?' I asked. 'Will your parents mind?'

'I'll ring Mum now,' Charlotte said. 'I know I said I was sorry we ever found Ice, but I'd really like to see what we can get out of him. I mean where did he come from? How did he get into the meteorite crater? What does he want?'

'You'd better not touch Ice,' Jun Mo warned as he got out his mobile to text his parents that he was coming home with me. 'He's already caused enough trouble.'

By the time we got home we were starving, so I raided the fridge and handed round bread, cheese and tomatoes which Charlotte and I made into sandwiches while Jun Mo scoffed his down whole.

'Come on,' I said as soon as we'd finished. 'Let's go and see if Ice is still rooted to the spot.'

Charlotte giggled and we all trooped down the garden to the shed.

It was difficult pulling the door open; it was as if something was holding it shut on the other side. We took turns wrenching at it and at last it flew open with a crash. We saw at once what had caused the problem. The abundant plants and creepers had latched onto the wooden door itself and little broken pieces of greenery were still hanging there.

'I hope that wasn't Ice,' Charlotte said, looking at the severed pieces of plant. 'We might have pulled an arm or a leg off or something.'

The plant Ice had transformed into the night before didn't seem to be there, although it was difficult to tell with all the tangles of new greenery inside the cramped shed. 'Ice?' I called anxiously. 'Ice, are you here?'

'He's not going to answer,' Jun Mo said. 'Ice can't speak.'

'Yeah, I know,' I said, feeling a bit stupid. 'But where is he?'

Charlotte was hanging back near the door. I knew she didn't want to come into contact with Ice by mistake and end up having to look at a pale, mute and probably naked version of herself. Jun Mo and I scoured the shed, touching as many plants as we could in the hope of finding him suddenly transforming in front us, but nothing happened.

And then Charlotte gave a strangled yell, and we turned to find her standing in front of the door with her arms out in a sort of cross.

'Don't look!' she cried, and of course we both looked to see a mirror image of Charlotte, peering timidly out from behind her shoulder.

'Here,' I said, ripping my shirt off quickly and thrusting it at her. 'Cover him…her, with this.'

'Turn your backs,' she demanded, and Jun Mo and I turned away while Charlotte dressed Ice in my shirt and buttoned it up to its neck again.

'Okay, he's decent,' she said wearily. 'I just can't believe it. I only rested back against the door frame and there he was, camouflaged as part of the shed itself. I thought you said he was rooted to the spot, so what happened?'

'His plant must have continued to grow and fallen against the wall of the shed,' I said, 'And then he was able to become the wooden panelling of the shed wall. Crikey! We *could* have pulled him apart when we opened the shed door just now. Lucky he was only part of the door frame and not the door.'

'If he can do that,' said Charlotte, 'what's to stop him becoming part of the outside wall…and then the path, and then the grass and the apple trees? What's to stop him disappearing into the rest of the world? We'd never find him again.'

'No wonder the people from the Space Agency are keen to hear reports of anything unusual,' I said. 'Perhaps they know that things like Ice can arrive here inside meteorites. They knew there was a meteor shower in this vicinity, so they're checking every strange occurrence in the area.'

'It must have happened before,' Jun Mo said slowly. 'That's why they know to look for green fingers. That's why the man came to school.'

We all looked at one another in dismay, while Ice stared at us in silence. Why was the Space Agency so keen to locate Ice? Was he the only one, or were there more of his kind hiding here on Earth?

'You don't think, do you,' Charlotte said quietly,

'that Ice is just one part of a bigger group: that there are Aliens hiding in camouflage all over our planet, waiting to invade?'

'I hope not,' I said, a bit nervous now about the whole thing. 'Otherwise we could be partly responsible for the destruction of the human race.'

Transformations

11

'I think you're being a bit over dramatic Will,' Charlotte said. 'Ice doesn't seem to be dangerous, does he? I can hardly believe he and his kind - if there are any more of his sort here - are going to actually try and annihilate us.'

'Space Agency man carried a gun,' Jun Mo reminded us. 'Maybe he thinks Ice is a big threat.'

We all stared at Ice who stood peering back at us cautiously. He looked so harmless standing there looking like Charlotte and buttoned into my school shirt.

'The trouble is I think you are right Charlotte. Although he seems to need to come into direct contact with something to take on its form, what's to stop him going from one thing to another in a sort of chain, until he vanishes into the rest of the world? And we don't know anything about him. What if he does turn out to be dangerous?' I said.

'What do you want to do then?' she demanded. 'Turn him over to the Space Agency so they can experiment on him, or even kill him? I for one didn't like the look of that man who came to school one little bit.'

'How do we keep him contained, though?' I asked, knowing Charlotte was right again. I hadn't liked the look of the Space Agency man either.

'Perhaps we could try and explain that he can't go wandering about,' Charlotte said. 'Just because he can't talk doesn't mean he doesn't understand us.'

She turned and stared deep into Ice's eyes, 'You mustn't wander off,' she told him. 'You have to stay here with me and Will and Jun Mo. It might be dangerous for you anywhere else.'

Ice merely stared back at Charlotte, mirroring her earnest expression.

'Ice doesn't understand,' Jun Mo said. 'What are we going to do?'

'Well, I'm going out into the sunshine,' Charlotte said. 'It's so dark and gloomy in here.'

She went towards the shed door and predictably Ice followed her.

'No,' she said patiently, as if she was talking to a small child. 'You have to stay here.' She turned to me and Jun Mo in exasperation. 'One of you come and distract him will you? I'm getting hot and thirsty and I want to get out of here.'

'I won't baby sit him,' Jun Mo said, following Charlotte to the door.

'This is stupid,' I said. 'If he can't be left safely, then we'll just have to keep him with us. Come on, Ice,' I said and the three of us trooped out into the warm sunshine with the second Charlotte at our heels.

The four of us went to sit in the shade of the apple tree. It was funny watching Ice sit on the grass, trying to copy Charlotte. The feel of the short spongy grass under his new body must have been strange, because I noticed he kept running his pale hands over the lawn as if feeling it for the first time and there was something else: for the first time he seemed to be making an expression of his own rather than one he'd copied from us. He was looking round at his surroundings with an interested look, whilst Charlotte was sitting with her eyes half closed.

'When's Luke coming home?' Jun Mo asked suddenly.

'I don't know. College breaks up today too, but he may not come straight home.'

'What do you think he'll make of Ice?' Charlotte murmured.

I shook my head grimly at the thought. 'He'll probably try to kill him.'

Ice seemed to be watching us in turn as if trying to make out what we were saying. It was strange seeing him and Charlotte together in the proper daylight. He looked like her and yet he was paler, more translucent, almost like one would imagine a ghost to be.

'Ice looks like a ghost,' Jun Mo said, echoing my thoughts. 'You think this is what a ghost is? Not a dead human at all, but an alien from a meteorite?'

Charlotte's eyes snapped open and she looked at Ice again with renewed interest. 'You know, you might have something there,' she said. 'If meteorites have been crashing to Earth since time and space began and people have reported seeing 'ghosts' for as long as anyone can remember, it seems quite possible that that is what ghosts really are...aliens, like Ice.'

'That's why they vanish,' Jun Mo continued enthusiastically. 'Ghost's vanish into a wall or door, just like Ice did in the shed.'

'Crikey!' I exclaimed. 'It certainly would explain a lot, like people who say they have poltergeists that move things around...hang on, do we know if Ice can pick things up or move them?'

Charlotte picked a tiny unripe apple off the grass and held it out to Ice.

We all watched as Ice held out his hand like Charlotte. But when she dropped the apple into his open palm, it fell through and landed back on the grass, where it rolled a short way before stopping.

'Weird,' I breathed, as Charlotte took Ice's hand in her own. 'We can feel Ice, like he's a solid entity, but he's not, is he? Blimey, did you see the way that apple just went straight through him?'

'Maybe the aliens *become* those objects that are seen moving around when people think they've got poltergeists in the house,' Charlotte suggested.

'Why's he not become an apple then?' asked Jun Mo.

I shrugged. 'Maybe Ice can choose what he mimics. And perhaps poltergeists have nothing to do with this at all,' I said. 'But I still think this could be what people see when they think they've seen a ghost.'

'Yes,' Charlotte said, her eyes shining with excitement. 'Maybe it all has to do with energy. Suppose Ice is just a ball of energy that arrived inside the meteorite? When he was floating in the puddle of water in the crater he didn't look like anything, did he? He was just a shining mass of energy...until he saw us. And then he touched you and transformed into a pretty good likeness of you, Will. And we know he can do it with plants and wood, and your cotton shirt, and of course me.'

She stopped to look at her double who was looking back at her with interest.

'All those things have cells...all natural things,' Jun Mo pointed out. 'Let's try with a man-made object.'

Scrambling to my feet, I ran back to the house to fetch an assortment of items, all of which I thought were big enough for Ice to transform into if he could. Jun Mo and Charlotte laughed when they saw me trudging back down the garden carrying a plastic chair from Dad's study, a metal clothes airer and a brass watering can.

Placing the items on the grass in the centre of the circle we had made under the apple tree, I looked from one of them to the other.

'Okay,' I said, panting slightly from my exertions. 'I reckon these are inanimate objects, don't you? They're not made up of living cells like wood and cotton and human flesh. Let's see what happens when Ice touches them.'

'Go on, try him,' Jun Mo said.

Holding out the chair towards Ice, I waited for him to reach out and touch it, but he just continued to look interested in what we were doing. Then Charlotte took his cold hand in hers and guided it towards the chair until Ice's fingers were resting on the plastic seat. We all watched expectantly, but nothing happened.

We tried again with the metal clothes airer and the watering can, but still Ice didn't transform.

'Maybe he just doesn't want to,' Charlotte said. 'It's not much of a test is it? We don't know if he can't transform into those things or if he just doesn't want to do it.'

'What about the path?' Jun Mo said suddenly. 'Let him stand on the stone path.'

We stood up and Ice stood up too. Then we all shuffled over to where the crazy paving path ran between the lawn and the shed and stood in a row on it. Ice stood with us looking hopeful, but he didn't suddenly sink down and become a paving slab like some sort of shape-shifter.

'I just had another thought,' I said as we trooped back to the shade of the apple tree with Charlotte's double following in our wake. We flung ourselves down onto the cool grass. 'What if he can only transform into things that have come into contact with the meteorite? So far he's been a likeness of me and Charlotte, who both touched the meteorite ice, the shirt I was wearing, a plant that grew out of the meteorite dust and the shed where the ice landed.' I turned to Jun Mo. 'You obviously didn't touch the meteorite as you're not green. Why don't you try touching Ice and see if he can turn into you?'

Jun Mo hung back, looking horrified.

'Go on,' Charlotte said. 'It doesn't hurt.'

Jun Mo reached out his hand slowly to Ice's and held his hand against Ice's pale green fingers and we all watched to see what would happen. Ice shimmered slightly, then his features began to swim before our eyes. His face changed shape first and then his body contorted: his shoulders and neck grew solid and his legs grew shorter and suddenly we were looking at a replica of Jun Mo, who was sitting glaring at us, still fortunately dressed in my school shirt.

I glanced at the real Jun Mo and found that Ice's expression was mimicking Jun Mo's own. 'That's that theory out then,' I said.

'It's a great pity really,' Charlotte said. 'Because with that theory Ice wouldn't have been able to leave the shed, well not unless he was being one of us. This means he can be anything as long as it's made from natural materials; as far as we know anyway.'

At that moment a shrill ringing tone erupted into the quiet afternoon air and Jun Mo scrabbled for his mobile 'phone. He listened intently for a moment then answered someone in rapid Korean. When he'd finished the call he looked at us with a grim expression on his face.

'That was my mother. She says the man from the Space Agency is waiting at my house for me. He told her he'd checked with the school for any unusual behaviour and they told him I was in a fight with those boys. Mr Jarvis told him I'm not normally trouble and the man wants to see me. I got to go home,' he stopped and groaned. 'Father will be very angry. I'm in big trouble now.'

I looked from Jun Mo to the second Jun Mo and shook my head. 'If the man from the Space Agency is on to you, it won't take long for him to find out that you were here with us on Saturday night. They'll come looking here next. You're not the only one who's in trouble, Jun Mo,' I said.

Hiding Out

12

'What are we going to do?' Charlotte asked. 'We can't let them find Ice. I couldn't bear it if they did anything horrible to him.'

'Well, we can't leave him on his own,' I said. 'And if he stays in the shed the man will definitely find him. What do you say to taking a camping trip; all three of us and Ice? Mum is going away for a few days on a training exercise and Dad's got a business trip and won't be back until next weekend. Why don't you both ask your parents if you can stay over and then we can clear off for a while and take Ice with us?'

'I'm sure Mum will let me stay over,' she said. 'But we'd have to get our stuff together, which means we've got to go home first.'

'I have to go home to face mother and that man,' Jun Mo said. 'Then I'll come back here with my sleeping bag tonight, okay?'

'Why don't we meet at the school at say, eight o'clock' I said. 'We can hide out in that old disused shed in the grounds.'

'My mum will have to drop me off here but I hope she doesn't want to speak to your mum', Charlotte said. 'She won't let me come if she knows your mum and dad are going to be away.'

'My parents better not ask; it's a bad thing to lie to your parents,' said Jun Mo.

'Yes,' I agreed, 'But it's that or let them take Ice.'

Getting Ice to stay in the shed while we got ourselves ready was impossible. We tried pushing him in several times, I even tried the old trick of draping a vine around him, but he simply squeezed out of it like a floating mist. He had obviously learned a thing or two in the last couple of days. Not only did he refuse to take on the shape of the plant, it wouldn't have done us any good anyhow, because he seemed also to have learned how to keep his form without being in close proximity to the thing he was copying. Jun Mo backed away and Ice stayed looking just like him, so I decided he had better come up to the house with me. As long as he stayed looking like Jun Mo, I reckoned no one would question his presence.

Jun Mo headed for the station to get the train to Guildford and Charlotte walked the mile or so back to her house to persuade her mother to let her come and stay at our house for a couple of nights.

I hurried up to my room with Ice at my heels, glancing back at him every so often to check he hadn't stopped to find anything more interesting to turn into on the way. Then Jun Mo Two sat on a chair with his hands resting on my computer, watching intently as I filled my rucksack with a change of clothes and found my tent and sleeping bag, which I'd used quite recently on a school trip, and which still had a dirty pair of socks rolled up at the end. Sniffing at them, I made a face and chucked them behind the bed.

I was halfway through picking some chewing gum off the bag's handle when Brutus sauntered into the room. The cat gave a friendly miaow; then stopped dead when he spotted Ice, and raised his hackles.

'Cat,' I explained to Ice. 'Cat says 'miaow'.' I turned to Brutus who had backed towards the door with his huge yellow eyes fixed on Ice. 'Don't be so daft, Brutus, Ice won't hurt you.' But Brutus had gone.

I lent Ice an old pair of my trousers and mimed putting them on, then told Ice to stay where he was while I crept down to the kitchen for supplies. Ice was having none of it; it seemed he craved company and wherever I went, that's where he wanted to be. So we were both in the kitchen when Luke came home.

'Hi Billy,' Luke said, knocking into me on purpose as he went past so that I spilled some of the orange squash I was pouring into a drinking bottle onto my feet. 'Hi Jun Mo.'

Ice of course, said nothing. Luke seemed to take his silence as a rebuke for having bumped into me.

'I love my little brother really,' he told Ice. 'Don't I Billy?'

'Yeah, you've just got a funny way of showing it,' I said. I didn't want a fight with Luke right now, not with Ice sitting there watching us. For all I knew he would start copying me or Luke if we started throwing punches and who knows what might happen. I couldn't help feeling that if Jun Mo, Charlotte and I were this much improved with our strength and intellect from sipping just a mouthful or two of the ice; the very same ice that Ice had been born from, then he could be very strong and pretty darn smart if he wanted to get started.

'Cat got your tongue, Jun Mo?' Luke said as he ambled past him.

'Cat say miaow,' said Ice.

Luke laughed and disappeared off into the playroom, but I stood there with my mouth open. It seemed that Ice had learned how to speak, or at least, he'd learned how to mimic sounds, and that could be something of a problem.

By the time Mum got in from work I had packed everything up and stowed it in the cupboard under the stairs.

'You will be alright, won't you?' she said an hour later as she picked up her training bag and headed for the car. 'There are plenty of ready meals in the freezer and I'm sure Luke will look after you. Don't forget to feed Brutus. Bye boys!'

'Bye Mum,' I called as she nosed the car out of the garage. Luke had come to wave her off and the three of us stood in a row: Luke and I waving and Ice watching the car go with a look of interest on his Jun Mo-like face.

As the car rounded a corner out of sight, Luke turned and smiled widely at us. 'Right,' he said. 'Now the coast is clear, I've got a few friends coming over, so make yourselves scarce.'

'Sure,' I said, in my best Jim Carey accent and returning his grin, 'Why not.'

Luke gave me a suspicious look, but then decided I wasn't worth his bother. He was just heading for the kitchen when the 'phone rang. I hurried into the kitchen to answer it, but Luke had got there first. He listened for a couple of seconds then said, 'Yeah right.'

He thrust the 'phone at me, giving Ice a wink, 'It's apparently Jun Mo, for you,' he said, holding out the 'phone.

'Oh,' I said, as the Jun Mo look-alike hovered at the kitchen door, 'Right, thanks.'

'Very funny,' said Luke as he went to the fridge and took out a six pack of lager he'd had hidden behind the fruit juice cartons. 'You can tell whoever it is on the 'phone that he didn't have me fooled for a second. He didn't sound anything like Jun Mo.'

I tried hard not to laugh as I took the 'phone from him. I was about to tell Jun Mo that Luke had said he didn't sound anything like himself, when my friend cut me short.

'You've got to get out of there,' he said urgently. 'My parents told the agency man I was with you and Charlotte on Saturday night. He's on the way to your house right now!'

After hurriedly replacing the receiver, I told Luke that 'Jun Mo' and I were about to go out and leave him in peace.

'About time too,' he said, 'and don't come back any time soon, my mates and I are having an end of term party and I don't want you or you little friends in the way.'

'Come on,' I said to Ice, 'We've got to go.'

Ice followed me to the under stair cupboard and waited while I found the rather overfilled rucksack and a small backpack, which I filled with a few extra things. I tried giving the smaller bag to Ice to carry, but it fell right through him and dropped onto the hall floor.

'Ouch,' I said, as I picked the things back up and stuffed them into the top of the rucksack, 'Doesn't that hurt?'

'Ouch,' said Ice with a grin.

Opening the front door carefully, I peered right and then left up our road but didn't see any unusual looking parked vans that could have had us under surveillance or any men in grey suits lurking in doorways watching us. Then I hurried down the road with Ice at my heels until we came to an alley that served as a short cut to the school.

At the entrance to the alleyway I stopped and glanced back at my house, just in time to see a group of teenage boys in jeans and hoodies standing on the doorstep. I knew most of them and they were clutching bags of what looked like cans of drink. I watched until the front door opened and they disappeared inside. Mum and Dad were not going to be very pleased when they got back, but there was nothing I could do about it. As far as they were concerned, Luke was a model son and I wasn't going to tell on him.

Ice and I walked on towards the school, where we said we'd wait for Jun Mo and for Charlotte to call and say she was on her way. Her parents would probably drop her at our house and I wanted to be back there so she didn't walk in on Luke and his mates. There was an old storage shed at the back of the school which was damp and leaking and had been abandoned a couple of terms before. Some of the kids hung out there sometimes, but I didn't think anyone would be there the day we'd broken up for the holidays; everyone would have had enough of the place for a while.

Ice and I pulled at a loose plank that covered one of the windows that had been boarded up; then I dropped the rucksack through the hole, climbed inside and helped Ice to climb in after me. It was weird when I held his wrist to pull him through, because although objects seemed to fall right through him, he felt solid to the touch. It was also odd that he felt cold instead of warm.

I propped the rucksack in the driest corner of the room, glad to get it off my back, then we sat against a wall and waited for Charlotte's call. Maybe half an hour passed and I occupied myself teaching Ice some more words. He was just repeating 'mobile 'phone' when the 'phone I was showing him rang, making me jump. Ice watched my reaction and then he jumped too, though rather late for it to look genuine.

'I'm on my way,' Charlotte said. Ice leaned towards the 'phone, seeming interested to hear her voice coming from it.

'We'll meet you outside the house,' I told her. 'Don't ring the bell because Luke is in there with a whole bunch of his mates.'

Ice followed me as I walked back towards our road through the alleyway. At the end of the alley we stopped and peered round the corner, making sure the coast was clear. As we watched, Charlotte's parents' car drew up outside my house and I hurried towards it, worried her parents might wonder why she wasn't ringing the bell.

'Hi Charlotte!' I called as she stood awkwardly on the pavement with her mother watching from the driver's side of the car. Charlotte had a small backpack on and was carrying a sleeping bag. She waved to me and started towards me and her mother turned, saw me and Ice – who she thought was Jun Mo - and smiled and waved before starting the car and disappearing off down the road.

'Come on,' I said, pulling Charlotte away from the house. 'Let's get out of here.'

We hurried towards the alleyway, but just before we headed down it, I heard the screech of tyres and looked back down the road…just in time to see a silver saloon car careering to a stop outside my house. We paused just inside the mouth of the alleyway and peered carefully back round the bushes, watching in dismay as three men in dark suits sprang from the car and began to hammer on the front door.

Canine Friend

13

'Quick! Let's go before they come looking for us,' Charlotte breathed, backing down the alley as the men banged loudly on the door a little way up the street. But I'd had another idea. I wanted to see what those men were going to do.

'Squeeze through the hedge here,' I said. 'Luke gets in and out this way when he's in trouble. We can crawl through the next four gardens without being seen and get right up to the wall that our shed backs onto. Come on, we can watch and listen from there.'

For a moment I thought Charlotte was going to refuse to come, but I reminded her about our extra powers, 'We'll be fine,' I told her, grinning at the thought of the adventure.

Climbing through small gaps in the hedges and crawling snake-like through gardens, slithering behind dormant bonfires, sheds and riotous runner bean plants, we were soon at the base of the wall that backed onto our garden. Ice seemed best at the slithering game, seeming to almost become one with the grass as he pressed his Jun Mo look-alike body along the ground. I smiled as he caught up with us; then turned my attention to the wall. Looking up, I could see the strange dark green shoots of climbing plants that had escaped through the hole in our shed roof and were now clambering about the top of the wall.

'What now?' whispered Charlotte.

'Now,' I said. 'We do the Luke special…watch.'

And I crept along the base of the shed, squeezing between a line of conifers and the fence itself until I was almost level with the back door of our house on the other side. The conifers hid us from our neighbour's view.

'But there's no way through,' Charlotte said as she arrived at my shoulder. 'The fence is solid.'

The wooden fence did indeed look solid, with trails of ancient ivy creeping here and there. But the ivy was in fact the key. Holding a particularly thick stem of the green and white plant, I pulled hard and a perfectly square section of the fence lifted out in my hand.

'Luke cut this hole out, and the ivy disguises the joins,' I said as I stuck my head through the hole and peered cautiously into my own garden. 'Sometimes he puts his empty beer cans through here if Mum or Dad get suspicious and go to search his room.'

'It can't be good for him to do all that drinking,' Charlotte said. 'Why does he do it?'

'Search me,' I said. 'Luke always thinks he's invincible.'

'What's happening? What can you see?' asked Charlotte as I gulped a quick intake of breath.

'It's those men; they're in the house, talking to Luke and his friends in the kitchen. The back door is open. Sssh! I think I might be able to hear what they're saying.'

For a while I stayed crouched, my head half through the low hole in the fence, staying back in the shadows so I wouldn't be seen while I listened to what was going on. When at last I drew my head back Charlotte was almost beside herself with frustration. 'What are they saying?' she said. 'Tell me!'

'They've told Luke that they are special enforcement officers and that they want to know where I am! Luke said I was out and they said they'd need to look right round the house and garden. Luke tried to stop them, but one of the men held up a can of lager and said if Luke and his friends didn't co operate fully, they would do them for under age drinking.'

'What's happening now?'

'I think they're in the house, searching for me...and for Ice probably.' I stopped and peered back through the gloom of the conifers for Ice. 'Where is he?'

Charlotte looked behind her in surprise. 'He was right here a moment ago.'

Panic surged through me at the thought of Ice wandering about in someone's garden on his own, just as the men from the agency were so closely on his trail.

'We've got to find him before they do. We can't keep him safe if we don't know where he's gone. Why weren't you keeping an eye on him?'

'Don't blame me,' Charlotte said huffily. 'I didn't know he was going to wander off.'

We started to wriggle back along the fence line, thinking to look for Ice in the neighbour's garden, when Charlotte gave a sudden screech.

'What is it?' I hissed from behind her.

'I can't get through, there's a tree blocking the gap. It wasn't there when we came through.'

'Let me see,' I said, squeezing round her. I prodded the trunk of the fully grown fir tree with my green finger tip and the trunk recoiled like a piece of rubber. 'Ice, is that you?'

There was no answer of course and I sat back on my heels with a groan. 'That's all we need. Ice has transformed into a flippin' tree just as we need him to be able to run as far and as fast away from those men as possible.'

'Can't we get him to transform back into Jun Mo again?' Charlotte asked. 'Whatever we do, it's got to be quick. I can hear people in your garden!'

'He can't transform into Jun Mo because Jun Mo's not here,' I said, thinking quickly. 'If we want Ice to be able to run, it's got to be one of us.'

'But then there'll be two of either you or me,' she hissed back, 'and that will look decidedly odd, won't it?'

I was trying to think what to do, when there was a crashing sound on our side of the fence and Charlotte and I both froze. The crashing was accompanied by heavy breathing and a sound as if someone was hitting the trees near us with some sort of beater. A wet, brown nose poked through the trees and I found myself looking into a pair of big brown eyes. It was the elderly Labrador dog from next door, only we were in his garden.

'Nice dog, don't bark,' I whispered as the dog's tail continued to slap against the trees as he wagged it happily. The dog pushed further through the trees until he was at eye level and I found myself breathing in a faceful of strong doggy smelling breath. His long pink tongue was hanging out and dripping saliva onto my jeans.

From the other side of the fence I could hear people talking.

'There's nothing out here, only the old shed,' Luke was saying. 'Have you got a search warrant or something?'

'We don't need a warrant, lad,' snapped an older male voice. 'Our agency has a licence to search any premises we want. And you don't have a licence for anything either, especially all that booze we've just confiscated.'

'I ought to call my parents,' Luke was saying. 'You could be anybody.'

'You go ahead and call them, lad. I can tell them what we found you and your friends doing. I'm sure they'd be delighted to hear about the other six boys lying around their house smoking, drinking and eating their food.'

'What do you want my brother for anyway?' Luke said. I could hear him panting as if hurrying to keep up with the man. 'What's he done?'

'Well if we could find him, we'd ask him,' the man replied.

They stopped on the other side of the fence where the shed nestled against the wall.

'What's in here?'

'Nothing,' said Luke. 'It's not been used for ages...except for a project my brother and his friends are doing.'

I tried to push past Ice, but he'd put himself bang in the middle of the crawl space, making it really difficult to get through. The dog was close behind me as I dragged myself past him, scratching my arms on Ice's rough trunk and low branches. The dog stopped dead when he came into contact with the tree and gave a low threatening growl.

'What was that?' asked the man next door.

'Next door's dog I should think,' said Luke. 'It's probably wondering what a stranger is doing, poking about in our garden.'

'Very funny, boy,' said the man. 'Open the shed.'

'It's not locked,' said Luke. 'Open it yourself.'

'I don't think I like your tone, lad,' said the man. And then I heard the shed door creak open and the man gave an excited shout.

'Here! Out here!' he yelled back to the other two men who were presumably still searching the house. 'I think we've got something!'

Charlotte and I crouched by the growling dog, trying to listen as more footsteps pounded down the garden next door.

'I knew it,' said a grating voice, a voice I

recognised. 'Those smart brats must have put the ink on their fingers to fool me. Well, I'm on to their little game now.'

It was the man who had given us the talk about comets at school. It was the horrible Temoc, and he was well and truly on to us.

'Get a cordon set up round this shed,' he instructed. 'And get the area sealed off. Those brats must be round here somewhere and when they come back, we'll get them.'

The Labrador gave a sudden startled whine and I turned round just in time to see him streaking off through the trees and across the lawn to his house. Charlotte was looking almost as startled as the dog, for there, sitting between us where the tree had been was a second Labrador, peering at me with big round eyes.

Helicopter Search

14

Charlotte and I hurried back the way we had come, through the other gardens, keeping as low as we could until we at last came to the hedge that bordered the alleyway with Ice bounding along at our heels.

'Quick, up the alley,' I called, and we ran as fast as we could while the sound of shouting and car doors slamming came to us from out in the road beyond the alley's mouth.

No sooner had we pelted into the road at the other end of the alley, than my mobile 'phone rang.

'Lucky that didn't happen earlier,' Charlotte said as we stopped, panting, and I pulled the 'phone from my pocket.

'What have you been up to little bro'?' came Luke's whispered voice. 'All hell has broken out here. I don't know what that little project of yours was down in the shed, but there are some mighty unsavoury characters here looking for you. You want advice from your big brother? Make yourself very scarce.'

'Thanks Luke,' I said quickly. 'If Mum or Dad ring, will you cover for me?'

'Already done little Billy,' said Luke in that joking voice of his. 'Mum isn't coming home for a few more days anyway; apparently she twisted her ankle almost as soon as she got out of the car and can't drive home. Dad rang to see if everything was cool and I told him it was. Man, this is *very* random; we have men from the ministry swarming about the place like headless flies. You'll have to tell me what it's all about as soon as you can.'

'Thanks Luke,' I said again. 'See you.'

By the time we got to the school storage shed, I realised it might not be safe to stay there after all. The men had come looking for something suspicious at the school in the first place and it might very well be one of the next places they looked for us now.

'We'll have to wait here for Jun Mo to join us, and then we'll move on,' I said as we pushed the board to one side of the window and climbed through the opening. Ice jumped in after us, trotted over to the rucksack and sat looking at us with his big Labrador eyes.

We waited for about twenty minutes in the gloom of the boarded up building and were eventually rewarded by a low whistle from outside. Ice pricked up his ears and trotted over to the window, looking up expectantly as the board was wrenched to one side.

'Jun Mo!' I said as he climbed through the gap and dropped down to join us, pulling his rucksack off his back as he did so. 'We're going to have to get out of here; those men from the agency are searching for us.'

'Hey you,' Jun Mo panted in greeting. 'I saw them already – there are men in suits knocking on doors all down your street. So; where are we going now?' He patted Ice absently as he spoke.

'Don't touch him!' Charlotte warned, 'Ice might turn into you again and it would look really odd if there was two of any of us. I know people might think we were twins, but we could bump into someone we know. Being a dog is quite a good disguise for him. No one would think it strange to see three kids with a dog.'

'This is Ice?' Jun Mo said in surprise.

'Yup,' I said. 'Look, I've been thinking while we were waiting for you. What about making our way to the Scout camp up on Timber Road? It's a few miles from here, but we can walk it easily with our new fitness levels. There's no reason they would look for us there, is there?'

'That's a good idea,' Charlotte said. 'I loved my week there when I was a Brownie.'

'I didn't know you'd been a Brownie,' I said.

'Well I didn't know you were a Scout,' she replied.

'We going then?' asked Jun Mo, obviously not understanding what we were talking about. I supposed they didn't have Brownies or Scouts in Korea.

'Did you see anyone suspicious anywhere near by?' I asked, sticking my head out of the boarded up window and looking around.

'No, it's all quiet,' Jun Mo said, 'Let's go.'

Charlotte and I divided up the equipment I'd brought and we carried a load each. Charlotte hadn't been able to bring more than her sleeping bag and a small back pack of bits and pieces as her parents thought she was staying at my house and it would have looked strange if she had set out with too much luggage.

'Did either of you bring any food?' I asked as we tramped along the dusty sun-burnt grass verge down a quiet tree lined road. It was late in the afternoon now and I was getting hungry.

'I've got some cereal bars,' Charlotte said. 'Do you want one now?'

Jun Mo and I both nodded and she stopped to rummage in the pocket of her jeans for three bars, which we unwrapped and ate eagerly.

'Did either of you bring money?' I asked as I swallowed the last mouthful and screwed up the wrapper. 'I was only able to find a few pounds in my room.'

Charlotte shook her head, but Jun Mo nodded. 'I've got plenty of money,' he said. 'I work hard, clean my parent's car and wash the windows every week. I've brought it all.' He unzipped the front pocket of his rucksack and held up a fistful of five pound notes.

'Wow! Well done Jun Mo. We'll need that for supplies. I've brought some food and drink but it won't last long. We'll pay you back, won't we Charlotte?'

Before she could answer, my mobile 'phone rang again. It was Luke.

'Look I don't know what the hell you guys have been up to, but its getting serious here. They've cordoned off the whole house and put barriers up in the road. They're stopping cars and questioning everyone who lives round here.'

'What about the shed?' I asked. 'What are they doing in there?'

'You'd have to see it to believe it,' Luke replied. 'They've brought in men in white boiler suits…you know the sort you see in films when there's dangerous substances, or they want to keep the area sterile…they're taking everything out of the shed in plastic evidence bags!'

'Crikey mate,' I said.

'Quit being a berk,' Luke said gruffly, 'what have you gone and done little bro'? Have you murdered one of your teachers and buried them out there? And what's with all the plants? It looks like Kew Gardens or the ruddy Eden Project in our back garden.'

'It's probably better you don't know,' I said wearily, suddenly realising that this was turning out to be more than an innocent adventure. 'If you don't know anything they can't get it out of you.'

'You're not telling me they might try torturing it out of me?' Luke said with some anxiety in his voice now. 'Blimey, I think I'd better have another beer.'

'Luke,' I said, lowering my voice and turning my back so that Jun Mo and Charlotte couldn't hear what I was saying. 'Are they armed, do you think?'

'I'm not sure,' Luke replied. 'But I don't think these guys are joking around, they won't let me or my mates leave the house. We're all sealed in like prisoners.'

'I'm really sorry Luke, but I've got to go. Keep me posted, okay?'

'Take care, squib,' said Luke.

'What did he say?' Jun Mo demanded when I turned back round to face them.

'They're swarming all over our house,' I told him. 'They're collecting everything from the shed in evidence bags.'

'Come on,' Charlotte said grimly. 'I think we'd better get ourselves off this road and hidden up at the camp site. There's still quite a long way to go.'

We arrived at the camp site an hour later to find it was already occupied by several Cub and Scout groups.

'Oh, no,' Charlotte said, dumping her bag and my equipment on the ground in the shelter of some trees where we were standing watching the scene before us. 'What are we going to do now?'

We watched the activity before us for a few minutes. The grassy open space between the surrounding trees was swarming with small uniformed children struggling with tent poles and equipment, and Scout leaders who were organising and unpacking canvas bags full of tents and hammers and poles.

'We could use this to our advantage,' I whispered. 'Who's going to notice three more kids amongst this lot? The only people who will know we don't belong here are the Scout leaders and we could tell them we are doing our Duke of Edinburgh Awards, couldn't we?'

'That's a good idea,' Charlotte said. 'Girls do that too, and we wouldn't need to be in uniform.'

'What is a Duke of Edinburgh Award?' Jun Mo asked as he rummaged in his back pack for something.

I often forgot that my friend had only been living in England for two years. 'It's a really cool sort of test,' I told him. 'You do hiking and camping and survival skills, and then you have to do community work and at the end you get a medal.' I explained.

'We're starting for real next year,' Charlotte put in. 'Are you going to do it too Jun Mo?'

Jun Mo pulled a bottle of water out of his bag and poured some into his cupped hand for Ice who was standing with his head down, panting; his tongue hanging out in the late afternoon warmth.

'I reckon we should get the medal now,' Jun Mo commented as the Labrador lapped eagerly at the water. 'We've just done the hike and now we're going to camp out and live off our wits...and we've saved this creature from bad men. That's the camping and survival skills *and* the community service taken care of!'

Charlotte was watching the dog with interest, 'You know, that's the first time we've seen Ice need to eat or drink anything. I never thought he might need to drink, I don't know why.'

'We don't even know what Ice is,' I pointed out. 'He must be something pretty special for those men to be scouring the area for him. Luke says they've got him and his friends under house arrest.'

'I'm surprised they haven't called your parents to come home,' Charlotte said, leaning her back against a tree, 'You'd think they'd want to ask them questions, if finding Ice is so important to them.'

'Maybe Luke exaggerated,' Jun Mo said as he wiped his hand on his trousers and hefted his bag back onto his broad shoulder. 'It looks pretty safe out there. Come on, let's go set up camp.'

Charlotte and I picked up our equipment, but Ice cowered back against the tree line.

'Come on, Ice,' I called as I started off across the grass. But the dog look-alike was pawing at his velvety ears and looking up at the sky.

'I think he can hear something,' Charlotte said. 'After all, he has got Labrador ears.'

And then we all heard what Ice must have been hearing; the wap, wap, wap of rotor blades and they were coming closer.

'Quick, back into the trees,' I cried, and we all scurried back under the shelter of the billowing trees as an army helicopter zoomed overhead with a deafening roar of whirling propellers and hurricane-like down draft.

The Camp Site

15

We crouched in the shadows, horrified, watching as Scouts and Scout masters alike dropped their tent poles and stood looking upwards at the hovering monster. I had never seen a helicopter so close up and the noise was almost unbearable as the rotor blades beat crazily at the sky above us.

Plastic carrier bags were whirled up into the air and dust rose in swirls as the down draft flattened the grass and knocked down the half erected tents. It seemed to hover there for an eternity, while we watched the black clad figures inside scouring the area with army binoculars.

'Keep down!' I cried, pulling Ice towards me and throwing myself on top of him in the soft pine needles. 'Get your heads down and keep very still!'

It seemed an age before the helicopter swooped sideways and rose into the air. The noise lessened as it swept away and I risked raising my face out of the pine needles to see it disappear into the distance, now no more than a speck of grey in the sky.

The camp site was a mess. We emerged from the

trees to find the Scout masters so busy consoling terrified children that they hardly gave us a glance as we found ourselves an empty space at the far end of the field and set about putting up our own tent with trembling hands.

'They had a gun,' Jun Mo said as I handed him the hammer. 'Did you see the gun inside the helicopter?'

'I didn't see a gun,' Charlotte said in a small voice.

Suddenly our adventure was turning a bit scary and I knew she was wishing she was safely at home with her parents.

Jun Mo smacked at the tent pegs with the hammer, his face grim. 'I saw a gun, a big gun. We're in real bad trouble.'

Later that evening when it was starting to get dark, we huddled together in the tent, trying to decide what to do. We had eaten a couple of tins of beans and sausage that I had brought with me in my rucksack and were now munching on some rather bruised apples. We had offered Ice some of the sausages, but he had hardly looked at them. It seemed he didn't need to eat after all.

'What is he, do you think?' Charlotte asked as she stroked Ice's floppy ears with one hand while she held her apple in the other. 'I mean, when we first saw him he didn't seem to be anything at all, just a blob floating in the puddle in the crater. It was only when he saw us that he started to look a bit human-like and since then he has been like a chameleon, changing his appearance to whatever he comes into contact with.'

'I think he *can* choose what he wants to be,' I put in. 'When I threw myself on top of him back there in the trees, he didn't turn into me again, did he? He seems to want to stay looking like a dog for the moment.'

'He's from space,' Jun Mo said, taking a bite of his apple and spitting bits out as he spoke. 'Maybe he's like a seed; come here to grow.'

Charlotte and I stared at Jun Mo, impressed. We had all learned about the theory of how life on Earth might have come from space, possibly from a meteorite, on a programme we had watched in a science lesson at school. It was one of the mysteries of how life began: an alien organism coming to our planet and seeding itself in the biological soup of Earth's early environment.

'We should have called him Adam then; not Ice,' Charlotte said. 'The bible says Adam and Eve were the first humans on Earth.'

'I think the organisms that originally came from space were a bit more basic than that.' I said, stopping to consider the core of my apple with its pips in the middle. 'I mean; blimey, it must have taken billions of years for us to evolve from something smaller than an apple pip to such complicated creatures as human beings.'

'Maybe Ice does not know what he should be.' Jun Mo said, shrugging his shoulders.

'You might have a point there, Jun Mo,' I said. 'Maybe that's why sometimes he changes and sometimes he doesn't.'

'Excuse me,' said a voice from outside the tent. 'I hope you don't mind me coming over, but we thought you might like to join our group for some hot chocolate and toasted marshmallows.'

I crawled over Jun Mo and Charlotte's legs, unzipped the tent flap and looked up to see a Scout master standing there in his smart uniform. He was an elderly man, with a grey moustache and glasses.

'You seem to be here without any adult supervision,' he went on. 'Is everything alright?'

'Er...yes, thank you. We're with that group doing our D of E expedition. We got a bit ahead of the others but I expect they'll be here any time.'

'Oh, right. What about that chocolate then? We've got a lovely camp fire going.'

I looked at Jun Mo and Charlotte and they both nodded enthusiastically, scrambling towards the entrance of the tent. It was then that the Scout master spotted Ice.

'Oh, you've got a dog with you, I'm not sure that is allowed, I'm afraid.'

'He can stay here in the tent,' I said. 'He's no trouble.'

'Well, as long as he doesn't run about or make a mess, I suppose we can overlook his presence,' said the man, smiling.

We stood up and he offered his hand for us to shake, 'Giles Peabody,' he said, introducing himself.

'I'm the science master at Oakcroft School. I run this Scout group in my spare time.'

'We're from Box Drake School, sir,' I said politely, wiping the sticky apple juice off my hands onto my jeans and shaking his hand back. I turned and zipped up the tent flap securely behind me so that Ice couldn't escape. 'Thank you for inviting us to join you.'

'No problem,' he said as we made our way over the field to where a group of eager looking Scouts had a good blaze going at their camp fire. 'I try to set the children a good example and do a good turn every day.'

One of the boys handed us sticks and another gave us a bag of marshmallows, so the next few minutes were occupied with skewering the marshmallows onto the sticks and toasting them over the flames.

'Here,' said Mr Peabody, handing us a plastic plate bearing biscuits and lumps of chocolate. 'Put a cube of the chocolate onto the biscuit, then hold your toasted marshmallow on the chocolate, slap another biscuit on top and pull the stick out from the middle of the sandwich, like this, look…and then eat.'

We followed his instructions closely. As the warm marshmallow melted the chocolate into a sweet gooey biscuit filling we started to eat and closed our eyes at the delicious combination; our situation as wanted fugitives momentarily forgotten.

'Now this is what I call camping,' Charlotte said, licking her lips and then her fingers. 'Are there more?'

We were about to spear another marshmallow each, when the group of boys nearest to us started to exclaim and giggle. Looking round, I saw a small golden Labrador stealing the marshmallow clean off the stick one of the boys had been holding.

'Ice?' I said.

'I thought your dog was shut in your tent,' the Scout master said. 'I saw you zip the flap shut. How on earth did it get out?'

'I…er…I'm not sure this is our dog, sir,' I said, studying the dog closely in the glow from the fire. 'It looks much smaller than ours…' I was about to add, 'and our dog doesn't eat,' but just stopped myself in time. What sort of dog didn't need to eat?

'Maybe we should go and check,' Charlotte whispered as she stroked the small dog's shiny coat, 'just in case.'

'Jun Mo and I can go,' I said, getting up from my cramped position on the grass by the fire. 'It's got really dark now and anyway you look like you're enjoying yourself.' I felt in my pocket for the torch I had had the foresight to bring with me and switched it on. 'We won't be long.'

As soon as we were out of sight of the Scouts, Jun Mo and I legged it across the field. It was still a novelty being able to run so fast and we raced each other to the tent, almost crashing through it because we could barely stop when we got there.

Jun Mo held the torch while I unzipped the tent flap.

'Ice?' I said, staring into the semi darkness.

Two bright orbs stared back in the torch light and Ice the Labrador came over to lie at my feet.

'Hi, Ice,' I said, patting him with relief. 'I'm glad you're still here.'

'Small problem,' Jun Mo said at my shoulder as he looked down at Ice, 'It's a small dog.'

'What?' I peered at Ice more closely and drew in a quick breath, 'Oh, no. I see what you mean. He's shrunk, hasn't he?'

Ice wagged his tail happily.

'Oh no,' I said, noticing a narrow tear between the side and front of the tent where it met the ground sheet. 'Do you think he's divided himself so he could slink through that gap and still stay here as well? Is it possible?'

Jun Mo shrugged, 'Cells divide; Ice is made of copied cells, so Ice could divide too.'

'Oh, great!' I said. 'This is all we need; two Ices' running around. This really complicates things. I mean, what if he can divide again and again and he gets smaller and smaller? He might be easier to hide, but what if we lose some of the bits? Will Ice cease to exist?'

'How did he get out of such a small gap?' Jun Mo said, crouching down to inspect the slim tear at the base of the tent. 'He must be able to become a very thin dog.'

'Go on, show us, Ice,' I said encouragingly. And to our great surprise, it seemed that not only had Ice learned to divide himself, he had also learned to understand some of what we said to him. He put his head on one side, as if considering what we wanted him to do; then he crawled towards the space. As he did so, he seemed to become one momentarily with the ground, almost as if he was made of liquid - much as he had done when we'd stolen across our neighbour's gardens earlier. Without actually losing his doggy identity, he became fluid, flowing smoothly beneath the tent and spilling out into the night air outside.

At that very minute my mobile 'phone rang somewhere at the back of the tent where I'd left it and I dived towards my rucksack and grabbed it up.

'Hello?' I answered breathlessly.

'Will? Is that you?' Came Luke's whispered voice.

'Yeah, how's it going Luke?'

'They've still got us locked up in here,' Luke said. 'They won't let us out. The house and garden are surrounded by plastic sheeting. They're telling everybody there is some sort of biological terror threat and no one's allowed in or out of the house. Dad 'phoned up again and they've told him not to come home! This is no longer funny, little bro'.'

'What do you mean; biological terror? What are they looking for exactly?'

'Well you're not going to believe this,' Luke said, 'but they're talking about a meteorite landing somewhere near here and apparently it had some sort of organism in it…something that could cause a world wide epidemic if it's not found and wiped out.'

I stared at the small Labrador who cocked his leg

against one of the tent pegs and then sat on the grass at my feet looking rather pleased with himself. Then I stared through the darkness towards the flickering camp fire where around fifty children were petting and playing with Ice's other half.

Turning to Jun Mo I felt almost dizzy with the horror of it all. What on earth had we done?

Lethal Disease

16

After zipping Ice Dog One securely back into the tent, Jun Mo and I raced back to the camp fire where we pulled the second dog away from the protesting children.

'I'm sorry,' I said to the Scout master. 'It is our dog after all...he just looked different in the fire light. We think he must have slipped through a tear in the side of the tent.'

'We'll have to hope it doesn't rain,' Mr Peabody said dryly. 'If there's a tear big enough for a Labrador to get through, you'd get pretty wet.'

I smiled politely at his joke, too anxious to get the second Ice as far away from the children as possible before they all caught some hideous plague from space. I was glad the green colouring on Charlotte and my hands wasn't visible in the dark. We were probably already infected.

Charlotte reluctantly put down her marshmallow and followed Jun Mo and me back to our tent, with Ice Dog Two trotting at our heels. 'What's all the panic about?' she said as soon as we were out of earshot of the camp. 'Anyone would think the poor dog was an escaped monster the way you two were treating him.'

'He might as well be,' I told her as we unzipped the tent flap and crawled inside dragging Ice Dog Two with us. 'I've just been speaking to Luke on my mobile and he says the men from the agency are treating our house and garden as if it infected with some lethal disease. They've told him about the meteorite and said there was an organism inside it... something that could cause a worldwide epidemic!'

Even in the yellow beam of the torch I could see Charlotte's face turn pale. She was staring at the two identical dogs and then down at her green tipped hands with fear in her eyes. 'Have we already got it?' she said. 'Do you think we could die?'

'Well, that's what Luke made it sound like,' I said, sinking down on my unrolled sleeping bag and pushing the second dog towards the one that was lying comfortably at the back of the tent. 'At least, that's what the men told him. They've locked Luke and his friends into house and won't even let my dad come home.'

'Look at Ice,' Jun Mo said, and Charlotte and I stared towards the two dogs who were now lying side by side. As we watched, the dogs crept closer to one another until one was virtually indistinguishable from the other; just a heap of golden fur with a busily wagging tail.

'Did I just imagine it or were there two dogs a moment ago?' Charlotte whispered.

'Ice divided like a cell,' Jun Mo told her. 'But it looks like he can get whole again.'

'I think I want to go home,' Charlotte said, groaning. 'I don't like this adventure any more.'

'The trouble is, we can't go home; we'll infect anyone we come into contact with,' I said. 'We can't risk giving it to our families.'

'We probably already have,' Charlotte said miserably. 'We've probably been contagious since we first touched the meteorite.'

'The whole school will have it then,' Jun Mo put in. 'We were at sports day and with the class at registration and lessons.'

'We didn't go out at break time though,' I said. 'Maybe we haven't given it to everyone yet.'

'Oh, yeah, only the whole Scout group here as well, and they'll go home and give it to their families and they'll give it to their friends,' Charlotte added. 'We might be responsible for the end of the human race.'

We sat in the cramped tent and stared morosely at each other and at Ice who was sitting watching us with his tongue hanging out. And then a thought struck me.

'Have either of you noticed that Ice seems to be learning stuff while he's here?' I asked. 'When he was at my house being Jun Mo he learned to say a couple of words. As a dog he's learned to drink water and to eat marshmallows and he certainly understood it when I asked him to show us how his other half got out of the tent just now. What if he can understand us? What if he could answer our questions?'

'If he says 'woof', we won't know what he says,' Jun Mo pointed out.

'Then he's got to take human form again,' I said, my eyes glowing with excitement. 'We'll have to explain to him that he has to become one of us, and then he may be able to speak to us. It is possible those men were lying to Luke about a biological threat, just so he'd give our whereabouts away. Ice might know if it's true or not, or what they really want him for.'

'He may be able to tell us where he came from,' Charlotte said, perking up a little at the thought, 'and what he's doing here.'

We all looked at Ice and then at one another.

'Who's it going to be then?' I asked.

We were saved from having to make that decision when a torch beam played on the entrance of the tent and we heard a deep voice asking to be let in. I opened the flap to allow Mr Peabody to duck inside.

'You went off in such a rush I didn't have a chance to give you these,' he said, handing Charlotte the remains of the bag of marshmallows. 'I noticed how much you were enjoying them,' he said with a smile.

I looked warily from the Scout master to Ice who was still lying with his tongue lolling out at the back of the tent. I wondered if I should have let Mr Peabody in; what if he got infected?

'You know, he does seem bigger, now I see him again,' Mr Peabody commented, staring fixedly at

Ice. 'I could have sworn he was a much smaller dog.'

'Probably a trick of the firelight,' I said, avoiding his gaze.

'Did you see that helicopter earlier?' Mr Peabody said, changing the subject suddenly.

I saw Jun Mo narrow his eyes suspiciously at the Scout master. I reckoned he was thinking the same as me, that it was a bit odd for Mr Peabody to walk right across the field in the dark just to give Charlotte a few left-over marshmallows.

'We heard it,' I said. 'It was gone by the time we arrived.'

'Ah, I thought I didn't see you when the helicopter was hovering,' he went on. 'It seemed like it was searching for something...or someone.'

'Really?' said Charlotte in a small voice.

'Yes,' said Mr Peabody. 'It gave us all quite a scare. But it obviously didn't find what it was searching for.'

We all looked at him, wondering what he was getting at. Could he possibly have guessed it was searching for us?

'The thing is,' he went on. 'I had the radio on earlier, and it said something about some missing children. He peered at us in the light from his torch and raised one eyebrow. 'I don't suppose it could be you?'

'We're not missing,' I pointed out. 'We're right here, and we're doing our Duke of Edinburgh Awards.'

'You look a bit young to be doing that already

and you should be accompanied by a leader. That makes me suspicious, so is there anything you want to tell me?'

'There's nothing we want to tell you, Mr Peabody,' Jun Mo said, evading Mr Peabody's probing. 'But as you are a science teacher, can I ask you a question?'

Mr Peabody nodded cautiously, 'Go ahead.'

'What does it take to say something is alive...really alive as a living being, not just a copy or a jumble of molecules?'

'Good heavens,' Mr Peabody said, taking off his glasses and cleaning them up on his handkerchief before answering. 'What a wonderful question! I wish some of my students would ask questions like that. What do you want to know for?'

'Just do,' Jun Mo said, darting a furtive look at Ice.

'Well now,' said Mr Peabody, settling himself on the edge of Jun Mo's sleeping bag, his anxiety about the missing children apparently forgotten. 'If you really want to know, then I can tell you that there are seven life processes which show something is alive. All plants and animals do these seven things. If something doesn't do all seven, then they're not considered to be alive.

I glanced across at Ice who was sitting up now, scratching at one of his ears with a shaggy back paw and wondered if he was listening. I wondered vaguely if scratching was one of the seven things.

'The seven things in question are; Movement,

Reproduction, Sensitivity, Nutrition, Excretion, Respiration and Growth,' Mr Peabody said, beaming round at us. 'Use this little trick to remind you of the first letter of each word: MRS NERG.'

'Mrs Nerg!' Jun Mo said. 'Mrs Nerg sounds like Mrs Nerd.'

I was just thinking that it was quite clever, but then I'd liked the rhyme about the kings and queens of England and look where that had got me.

'Well I think it's a very good way of remembering,' Charlotte said. She was looking at me meaningfully. 'Do any apply?' she mouthed silently at me.

I ran the seven life processes through in my head. Movement...well yes, Ice could certainly move. Reproduction...did being able to divide into two count? Sensitivity...well, I wasn't sure. 'What do you mean by sensitivity?' I asked Mr Peabody.

'It means responding to the outside world,' he replied.

I thought about it. Ice responded to the outside world by camouflaging himself to things he came into contact with so I supposed that did count. Nutrition, well, hadn't he just stolen a marshmallow? And I was pretty sure he'd swallowed it. As for excretion...I remembered seeing one of the Ice Dogs cock his leg against the tent pole, so he had done a wee. Respiration? Did Ice breathe? I watched the Labrador panting in the corner of the tent. Yup, I thought, he was certainly breathing, so that just left growth. Did Ice grow? Well he had grown pretty enormous when he was a tree, and he grew when the two dogs got back together, so that was that. Ice was a living creature.

I realised everyone was looking at me, including Mr Peabody.

'Any other little scientific questions you'd like to ask me?' he said hopefully.

'Is it possible for something alive to change into something else?' I asked.

'What do you mean exactly?' he said, peering at me through his glasses. 'Things change when they grow of course…a cygnet turns into a swan; a caterpillar turns into a butterfly…that sort of thing.'

'I mean at a more basic level sir, er… molecules and atoms and that sort of stuff,' I said.

'My goodness! What school do you chaps go to? You certainly have very enquiring minds.'

I noticed that Ice had stopped scratching and had squeezed his way to where the scout master was sitting and was now pressing up against him so that Mr Peabody had no choice but to take some notice of him. He patted him absently while he though of the answer to my question, quite unaware that the subject of our discussion was under his very fingertips.

'Well, everything in our world including the planet Earth itself and everything outside the world in space is made of atoms,' he said at last. 'Not all atoms are the same; the different kinds of atoms are called elements, the most common of which is hydrogen. Most living things are made of the carbon, hydrogen and oxygen atoms... and atoms link together to make molecules. Most of a human body's mass is made up of the elements oxygen, carbon and hydrogen.

Jun Mo yawned rudely and I flashed him a fierce look. It might sound boring, but we needed to know if Ice was some sort of contagious germ or if he was just a natural phenomenon.

'So can these carbon based molecules change?' I pressed.

'Some elements can exist in different physical forms and carbon *is* one of them,' Mr Peabody continued, nodding. 'If carbon atoms are squashed near together they form diamonds; one of the hardest substances on earth, but if they are spaced further apart they make soft lumps of coal or graphite. Burning can bring about change – it happens when molecules break apart to release their atoms and then the atoms join together in new combinations.'

'What about living things?' I asked, trying to get him back on track.

'One very important group of molecules is the carbohydrates,' Mr Peabody explained. 'Most people think of carbohydrates only as something we eat but they always contain atoms of the elements carbon, hydrogen and oxygen too, just like our bodies.'

'Are marshmallows made of carbohydrates, Mr Peabody?' Charlotte asked, popping one into her mouth.

The scoutmaster nodded. 'They are indeed. Carbohydrates include sugars, starches and dietry fibres, but they are still composed of…'

'Carbon, hydrogen and oxygen,' Jun Mo droned, as if he knew it all already.

'Yes,' nodded Mr Peabody. 'And carbohydrates taken in by the body are used for or change into…energy.'

'So if something was made of the basic elements like carbon, hydrogen and oxygen, they could form all sorts of different things?' I asked excitedly.

'Yes, but only with a pattern to follow and that pattern is a genetic code called DNA which is present in all living things. The DNA molecule gives the instructions as to what something will look like and behave like.'

So, I thought; if something came from space made from the basic elements of life and they could somehow read and then mimic or copy the DNA of living things they came into contact with, they could maybe somehow *become* those things.

Jun Mo suddenly reached over and grabbed Mr Peabody's torch and Charlotte gave a scream as the tent was plunged into darkness. For a moment everything was chaos as somebody squeezed over me, there seemed to be legs and arms flailing everywhere. I felt a draught as if someone had opened the tent flap, and in the faint moonlight I could have sworn I saw Mr Peabody leave the tent. Then everything went quiet again.

'What the devil's going on?' Mr Peabody demanded.

Jun Mo turned the torch on again and shone it

round the tent. Charlotte was clinging to his other arm, her eyes wide with fright. Mr Peabody was wiping his brow with his handkerchief looking rather disconcerted.

And Ice had vanished.

Mr Peabody

17

'What's going on?' Mr Peabody repeated, blinking owlishly round the tent in the restored torch light.

'I saw a spider crawling on your torch,' Charlotte said shakily. 'Jun Mo knows I hate spiders.'

'And where's the dog?' Mr Peabody said in a puzzled voice. 'Has he slipped out through that tear again?'

'I think he must have escaped while Jun Mo was dealing with the spider,' I lied, thinking quickly as Jun Mo flashed me urgent glances.

'Ah, well, as long as you're all alright, I'd better get back to my charges,' Mr Peabody said looking a bit bemused as he crawled towards the tent flap. 'I have to say I am still a little concerned that the rest of your D of E group has failed to arrive. I'm sure you'll be quite alright here tonight, but if they have not made contact with you by the morning I will have to call your parents. And if any of you have any confessions to make, I'd be pleased to hear them. The parents of those missing children must be worried sick.'

'Goodnight sir,' I said as he stood up and stretched outside the tent. I wanted to say, 'and thank you for not reporting us tonight', but contented myself with; 'And thank you for the scientific information, sir.'

And the information he had given us had been invaluable. We now knew two important things; one that Ice was truly alive and secondly that his ability to change from one thing to another was scientifically possible. At least we knew we weren't dreaming or going mad, anyway.

We watched as he made his way back over the field, his torch beam swinging across the dark grass, then Jun Mo turned to me and grinned.

'Ice turned into Mr Peabody!' He giggled. 'Just as he said 'the DNA molecule gives instructions on what something will look and behave like', Ice copied Mr Peabody's DNA and whoosh, he was Mr Peabody!'

'So there wasn't really a spider?'

Jun Mo shook his head. 'Charlotte made that up to explain why I'd grabbed the torch.' He looked slightly disapproving of her having lied to a teacher, but then he must have remembered that he'd been less than truthful himself when Mr Peabody had asked him if we were the missing children, because he suddenly grinned again. 'That was clever thinking,' he said.

I peered round into the darkness to see if I could catch a glimpse of Mr Peabody's double, but there was no sign of him.

'I hope he hasn't gone over to the Scout tents,' Charlotte said, looking rather pleased with Jun Mo's unaccustomed praise but then shivering suddenly in the cool night air. 'He'll get into all kinds of trouble, not to mention passing on the infection to all those children.'

'I don't think Ice is contagious,' I said thoughtfully. 'I think the Space Agency men are just saying that to scare Luke into giving away our whereabouts. From what Mr Peabody told us, I think the meteorite had the raw elements of life inside it and when it melted, it just left Ice floating in that puddle, waiting to decide what to become.'

'Do you think that's why we are suddenly so clever and so fast?' Charlotte said as we returned to the warmth of the tent. 'Because we actually drank some of that ice-stuff in our cokes, we've kind of soaked up some extra life energy?'

'It's possible,' I said, nodding. 'And the men from the Space Agency or whoever they really are, either want to capture him to use his energy for their own ends, or else they are scared of what they don't understand and want to destroy him.'

'People are scared of anyone different,' Jun Mo put in. 'A few people I come across are mean to me because I'm Korean and I'm human just like them. So if they can be that mean to another human, then I feel very sorry for poor Ice.'

'What are we going to do?' Charlotte asked. 'My parents must have heard what is going on at your house by now and be worried sick, just like Mr Peabody said.'

'I'm surprised they haven't rung your mobile,' I said. 'Luke has been ringing me.'

'I think the battery is flat,' she said, pulling the 'phone from her pocket and holding it in the torch light. 'Look, it's completely dead.'

'Look, it's completely dead,' echoed a deep voice from somewhere just beyond the tent. We all snapped our heads up, listening.

'It's Mr Peabody,' Jun Mo whispered. 'I bet it is Mr Peabody Two!'

'If it is Ice, then you were right about him learning to talk,' whispered Charlotte. 'Are you going to look outside?'

I contemplated my answer. Somehow the Ice dog hadn't seemed so bad. Having an adult human-looking Ice was unnerving to say the least.

'I suppose now we'll find out if he's dangerous,' I said as I crawled towards the tent flap. 'He couldn't do much harm as one of us, or a tree, or a dog. Let's hope he hasn't turned into the mad axe man.'

'Don't!' Charlotte shrieked, grabbing my arm. 'Don't say things like that. We're in the middle of a field in the dark and no one knows we're here. Anything could happen to us.'

'Mr Peabody would save us,' Jun Mo said.

'Oh yes? Well he'd be a bit shocked to find himself grappling with *himself* if he had to run over to save us,' Charlotte said with a sniff.

I unzipped the tent flap and peered out into the dark night. I could still smell the wood smoke from the smouldering remnants of the camp fire across the field, but the flames had died down and I could no longer make it out; or the cluster of Scout tents a little further off. It occurred to me that Charlotte was right…anything could happen to us and nobody would know what had happened.

'Ice?' I called. 'Are you there?'

A shadow loomed towards me and I drew back stifling a yell. Apart from the fact that I didn't want the other two to think I was a complete coward, I also didn't want the real Mr Peabody to come running over. Well, not yet anyway.

'Ice?' I whispered, looking up. 'Is that you?'

'Is that you?' said Mr Peabody Two crouching down beside me and staring into my eyes with interest. I realised Jun Mo was shining his torch on us both, because I could make out Mr Peabody's features despite the darkness. Only Mr Peabody Two wasn't wearing glasses. In fact he wasn't wearing anything at all.

'Oh, no,' I groaned. 'Jun Mo, get my spare trousers out of my back pack, will you? Mr Peabody hasn't got any clothes on.'

I heard Jun Mo rummaging about in the back of the tent and then he joined me in the doorway, grinning.

'Here, put these on, Ice.' He said, holding out a pair of jeans.

Ice stared at the trousers with interest, but didn't take them. I remembered that when he had turned into each of us we'd had to mime how to put the clothes on. I wondered why he hadn't learned how to do it by now, but then each time he'd changed, his energy had inhabited a different brain. I wondered if each time he became something he had to learn everything all over again. Maybe that's why he had snatched the marshmallow when he'd been the dog…it was something the pattern of the dog's brain had allowed for.

I quickly mimed putting the trousers on, after all we could hardly leave Ice out there looking like a naked Mr Peabody; if one of the Scouts should see him the poor man would be hauled up on charges and probably lose his job. Who was going to believe it wasn't Mr Peabody running round naked when he looked exactly like him?

I held the jeans out to Ice again and after a moment Ice took them. Jun Mo and I turned our backs while he got dressed.

'Come inside,' I said, beckoning Ice into the tent, 'We've got to talk.'

'We've got to talk,' Ice repeated as he ducked in after us and sat on Jun Mo's sleeping bag just as the real Mr Peabody had done only a short while before.

'Here, put this on,' Charlotte said to Ice, holding out the baggy sweatshirt she'd had tied round her waist. 'You can't sit there with a bare chest, you'll get cold.'

'You'll have to show him how,' I said.

Charlotte pulled the sweatshirt over her own head, pushed her arms into the sleeves, took it off again and handed it to Ice. He pulled it on as if he had been doing it all his life.

'Ice is a quick learner,' Jun Mo observed with a chuckle, 'he's got Mr Peabody's brain now. Maybe he can tell us where he comes from and what he is.'

'Can you?' I asked, looking into Ice's pale blue eyes. 'Can you tell us where you're from?'

'Can you tell us where you're from?' Ice repeated in Mr Peabody's voice, looking rather pleased with himself. I noticed he rolled the words around in his mouth as if he was testing the flavour of a new ice cream. He seemed to be enjoying being able to talk, but then he just stopped and sat looking at us.

'Who are you?' Charlotte asked. She pointed to herself and said, 'Charlotte.'

'Charlotte,' Ice repeated.

'And this is Jun Mo.'

'Jun Mo,' Ice said slowly, dragging out the 'O' sound as if he were savouring the sound.

'I'm Will,' I said.

'Will,' Ice repeated slowly.

'And you are…?' Charlotte prompted, pointing at his chest.

Ice put his head on one side and stared from one of us to the other, and then he opened his mouth and said, 'Ice.'

'He answered us!' Jun Mo said excitedly. 'He's learning all the time.'

'That's just the name we've given him,' Charlotte said, 'I'll bet he's only said it because that's what we keep calling him every time we see him. He's just copying what we say.'

'Maybe he hasn't got a name,' I said. 'If he's not

normally human, he might not have one of his own.'

'What are you doing here Ice?' Jun Mo said, ignoring me. 'Why have you come to Earth?'

'Earth?' repeated Ice looking puzzled.

Crawling past the other two, I went to my back pack and took out a small notebook and a pen. Then I drew a circle which was supposed to look like the sun and nine smaller and larger circles in a line beside it representing the nine planets in our solar system. I pointed to the third planet from the sun, 'Earth,' I said, watching Ice closely for a sign that he understood. I patted the ground beneath the tent floor and said it again, 'Earth.'

Ice nodded, looking interested again. 'Earth,' he repeated, but this time he was nodding and smiling.

Sighing, I sat back on my haunches and contemplated Ice thoughtfully. 'I'm not sure if he's simply mimicking the words or whether he's actually learning them,' I said.

'Okay,' Charlotte said suddenly, 'Let's assume he's learning them, after all, as Jun Mo said, he's got Mr Peabody's brain – or a replica of it anyway. Let's try teaching him some more words and then he might be able to use them to answer our questions.'

'Good idea,' Jun Mo said, leaning towards Ice and pointing to his chest, 'You look like Mr Peabody. Try to use his brain, okay?'

Jun Mo scrambled to the entrance of the tent and pointed out into the darkness the way Mr Peabody had gone. 'Mr Peabody...he's the Scout group leader. He's gone to join his group.'

Charlotte giggled, 'It would be funny if Ice learned to speak with a Korean accent,' she said.

'It would be funny if he learns to speak at all,' Jun Mo retorted.

They glared at one another for a moment and I hastily changed the subject, taking the pen and drawing more stars and suns around the picture I'd already done of our solar system.

'Where do you come from Ice?' I asked for the second time that evening. I expected him to repeat what I'd said, but instead, he reached out a green tipped finger and pointed to a place in the middle of the stars I'd drawn.

'Ice come from,' he said.

We all looked at him expectantly, but Ice didn't say anything else, he just sat and looked expectantly back at us.

'I bet he doesn't know the word for where he's from,' Charlotte said. 'Let's try this instead. What are you here for?' she said pointing to Ice and then to the picture I'd drawn of the Earth. 'Why?'

Ice stared at Charlotte intently for a moment then said, 'Ice join group.'

'Wow!' Charlotte said, her eyes bright with excitement. 'He's said something of his own.'

'He's just using words I told him about Mr Peabody,' Jun Mo said.

'Yes, but he's using them in his own way, not just copying the sounds we make,' I said. I felt as excited as Charlotte looked. Taking the pen again I drew a rough sketch of the United Kingdom. 'Where is your group?'

Ice stretched out his finger again and pointed to an area I didn't recognise to the south west of us.

We spent the next couple of hours drawing pictures and teaching Ice new words and we found out that Ice was indeed a fast learner. At the end of it he could tell us three important things. One was that he was not alone; each of the meteorites in the meteor shower had the potential for life hidden within its outer core. The second was that these showers had been coming to Earth for a very long time, maybe since the beginnings of the planet itself.

When we'd pressed him about why this happened, he'd simply said that he was part of the energy that created new life, wherever it was needed.

'So he is an alien,' Charlotte said, yawning widely. 'And there are lots more of them wandering about. No wonder the men from the Space Agency want to find him.'

'Crikey!' I said tiredly. 'If he's the energy that made life on this planet, then that probably makes us aliens too.'

Stolen Energy

18

The third thing Ice managed to convey to us – and it was even more worrying than the fact that all life on Earth had probably come here from space, was that Ice had a problem. I hadn't handed him the pen at first because I thought, like the apple in our garden, it would simply fall through his loosely flowing atoms and drop to the floor. I hadn't reckoned on the fact that like when we touched him and could feel him, or like the fact that his clothes didn't simply fall through him into a heap on the ground, he could somehow tighten his energy up and make himself feel almost solid when he needed to.

After over an hour of the three of us drawing him pictures and saying the words so he could learn them, Ice leaned forwards and took the pen out of my hand. We all watched, agog, as he drew a circle.

'Maybe it's a planet,' Charlotte breathed. 'He's going to show us where he's from.'

'No, he's cutting up the planet,' Jun Mo said in a puzzled voice as we watched Ice divide the circle up rather like slices of cake. He'd drawn one half of the cake uncut, but the other half he'd shaded in ink. Out of this section he cut three thin slices with the pen, leaving the other three quarters of the shaded section blank. Ice then sat back and looked at each of us in turn.

'Ice,' he said, pointing at the big uncut half of the cake. 'Will,' he said pointing to one thin slice of the cut cake. 'Charlotte,' he said pointing to the second slice and 'Jun Mo,' when he pointed at the third slice of the cake. That just left the other chunk unaccounted for.

We all stared at Ice, not really understanding what he meant, then Charlotte burst out, 'Oh no!'

'What?' Jun Mo demanded. 'What's he mean?'

'I think the whole circle represents Ice's energy mass as he fell to Earth,' Charlotte explained. 'But then we cut it up, didn't we? We chipped great lumps off the dirty ice and Luke made us drink some of it. That means some of the energy Ice needed to be whatever it was he was supposed to be went into each of us...that's why we suddenly got clever and stronger and everything!'

'So do you think that's why he's still here with us?' I asked. 'He's staying close to us because he needs his energy back?'

'Probably,' Charlotte said, nodding. 'We've stolen some of his life force and he can't do his job properly without it.'

'Blimey,' I said.

'Uh oh,' Jun Mo said quietly. 'What about the last chunk of cake?'

I pictured the empty freezer bags in the sink and groaned, 'It's what we hid in the freezer...only Luke threw it down the drain!'

We sat in a tired circle solemnly contemplating Ice.

'I'm really sorry,' Charlotte said, giving one of Ice's cold hands a squeeze. 'If we could give it back to you, we would.'

'Ice must join group,' Ice said quietly. He pointed to the sketch I'd made of the UK and jabbed his finger at that area to the south west again.

'Look, we'll try to get some sleep,' I said. 'And in the morning we'll pack up and head south with Ice. What do you think?'

Jun Mo and Charlotte nodded and we spread out our sleeping bags while Ice watched us sadly.

'He won't try to kill us in the night will he?' Charlotte asked anxiously as she snuggled down in her bag. 'I mean, if he killed us, maybe he could get his energy back from us.'

'No, Ice won't hurt us, will you Ice?' I said with more conviction than I felt. 'He could have hurt us at any time since we found him if he'd wanted to, couldn't he?'

'Ice not hurt you,' Ice said softly.

And with that reassurance, we all fell fast asleep.

The next morning we were woken by the shrieks of the Scout group playing a game of tag across the field. I opened one bleary eye to find Ice still sitting morosely where we'd left him the night before and I struggled out of my sleeping bag wondering what to do about breakfast.

'Jun Mo, can we have some of your money?' I asked as he stuck his dark head out of his bag and blinked in the strange green light that was filtering through the tent wall. He pulled his back pack towards him and pulled a couple of five pound notes from the front pocket.

'What are you going to buy?' he asked.

'Anything they'll sell me,' I replied with a grin. 'See you in a minute.'

Ice rose to his feet and I realised he was trying to come with me.

'No Ice, you can't come,' I explained. 'There can't be two Mr Peabody's wandering about.'

Ice glanced at Charlotte who was just sitting up and stretching.

'You can't be Charlotte either,' I told him, guessing what he was thinking. 'It will be much better if you stay as Mr Peabody for when we leave here later. The Space Agency people are looking for three unaccompanied children, not a family group with an adult.'

Ice sank back down on the ground again and I felt really mean as I left the confines of the tent, walked out into the glorious sunshine of a late July day and sauntered across the grass towards the Scout encampment.

I could smell bacon cooking as I drew closer and found the real Mr Peabody hunched over a camping stove, frying bacon, eggs and sausage. He started as I came up behind him but smiled when he saw who it was.

'Hungry are you?' he asked, banging a spatula thing against the side of the pan.

'Yes. I was wondering if you would sell us some of your food. I've got money,' I said, showing him the five pound notes.

'No need for that lad,' he said, tipping out some of the food onto a plate and adding a couple more rashers of bacon to the pan. 'Tell your friends to come over here and you can share what's left. The boys have already eaten.'

'Great!' I said. 'I'll go and fetch them.'

When I got back to the tent the others were up and ready to come for breakfast. We looked at Ice dubiously, unsure if he needed to eat or not.

'Do you need food?' I asked him, miming putting something in my mouth and chewing. 'Are you hungry?'

Ice shook his head. 'Not need food,' he said. 'Need to join my group.'

'We'll set off to find them as soon as we've eaten, I promise. You will stay here won't you?' I asked over my shoulder as Charlotte, Jun Mo and I headed off over the field. 'Don't wander off.'

'I stay here,' Ice said quietly.

Mr Peabody gave us three huge helpings of bacon, eggs and sausage, which we washed down with large quantities of orange juice.

'What are the three of you up to today, then?' he

asked as he watched us lick clean our plates. 'By the look of it you were all pretty hungry.'

'We're doing a walk,' I said. 'You know; the next bit of the D of E expedition.'

'I notice you are still on your own. Where are you headed? Have you got your maps with you? We could look over the route now if you like,' Mr Peabody said in a bit of a rush.

I glanced up at him, worried that he was being quite so helpful. I knew he was suspicious of us, and now he wanted to know where we were headed. Suddenly the delicious breakfast he had made us took on the feeling of a condemned man's last meal. Had he already reported us? I wasn't sure. 'We've got the route all planned, thank you sir,' I said politely, handing him back the empty plates and getting to my feet. 'And thank you for breakfast.'

'My pleasure,' he said as we turned away. 'Take care now.'

As we headed back across the field, Charlotte turned to look round and found Mr Peabody staring after us.

'He's definitely on to us,' she whispered. 'I think he'll tell someone he's seen us.'

'Or maybe he already has,' I said ominously.

'We'd better get away quickly,' Jun Mo agreed.

It was difficult not to break into a run across the field. We all had so much pent up energy, but we knew Mr Peabody was watching and so we slowed to what seemed like a saunter as we kicked through the long grass and daisies, though we got back to the tent in no time at all. Fortunately Ice was still sitting there looking miserable.

As quickly as possible, we dismantled the tent and packed everything away in the rucksack and back packs, doing our best to shield Ice from prying eyes with our bodies as he sat on the grass watching us.

'Come on,' I said as soon as we were ready, 'time to go.'

We'd only just made it to the shelter of the trees when my mobile rang. I threw down my heavy bags and answered warily, 'Yes?'

It was Luke.

'Look, things are getting worse here, little bro',' he said. 'These goons are sticking needles in us and taking blood samples from anything that moves within a hundred metre radius of the house. They've even stuck Brutus and next door's old dog, poor thing. You should have heard him howl. What the devil have you been up to?'

I took a deep breath before answering. 'You know what they told you about the meteorite landing in our garden?'

'Yeah…I didn't believe a word of it, load of whackos, that's what they are.'

'Well it's true, Luke, honestly. A meteorite hit our shed and that's why all those plants sprouted in there.'

'Yeah, yeah, little Billy, pull the other one.'

'The meteorite had life inside it,' I ploughed on ignoring the fact that he obviously didn't believe a word of it, 'but it couldn't become what it was supposed to, because we'd taken some of it.'

'Uh huh,' he said vaguely.

'It was in that ice you made us drink and in the stuff you threw down the sink and now the creature we're calling Ice, hasn't got enough energy to do whatever it is he came here to do.'

'Very funny,' he said, but this time he didn't seem quite so sure of himself. He'd gone quiet on the other end of the 'phone.

'I wasn't going to tell you in case they tortured it out of you with truth drugs and things. But it sounds like they're putting you through a pretty bad time anyway.'

'Are you serious?' Luke whispered, his voice suddenly not sounding jovial at all.

'Deadly,' I replied.

'Look…about that ice,' he began. But I didn't hear the rest of his sentence because turning into the camp site car park at speed, was an unmarked silver car followed by what looked like an armed response vehicle with its blue light flashing.

The Train

19

We watched from the trees as the cars screeched to a stop, sending up clouds of brown dust. The three grey suited men that had gone to our house spilled out of the silver car into the car park quickly followed by five uniformed officers from the police vehicle, each carrying an automatic weapon over their shoulders.

'They've *definitely* got guns,' Jun Mo breathed beside me as the men hurried over to the gaping group of Scouts.

We could see that even the plain clothed officers had holstered guns quite clearly showing under their open jackets. We watched as a bespectacled Mr Peabody strode out in front of his terrified group of boys and talked to the men at length, pointing to the place across the field where our tent had been pitched only a few minutes before.

'He must have told someone about us first thing this morning,' Charlotte said indignantly. 'Come on, we'd better get out of here.'

'Wait a minute,' I warned, putting a restraining

hand on Charlotte's arm. 'Keep still, they're looking this way.'

The uniformed police officers stayed hovering in a group by their vehicle, apparently awaiting orders while the other men began to walk slowly towards the patch of trees where we were hiding. I knew that if one of us moved, they would spot us for sure.

'We've got to go,' Jun Mo hissed. 'They're coming over here!'

But at that moment a tan coloured shaggy dog appeared on the far end of the field and the men stopped in mid stride and stared at it. Mr Peabody had obviously told them we had a golden Labrador with us, and they watched it suspiciously for a moment before heading in the direction from which it had come.

A few seconds later the dog's owner, a teenage boy, wandered out onto the footpath that edged the field, the dog's lead swinging from his hand.

In unison the grey suited men drew their guns and aimed at the pair. The armed officers leapt into action, three kneeling while the other two stood above and behind them, covering the boy and his dog with the aimed weapons.

'Hold it right there!' Shouted one of the men loudly, 'we are armed officers; put your hands where we can see them; now!'

The boy stopped dead in his tracks, his mouth dropping open in disbelief.

'Hold onto the dog!' shouted another of the men. 'Keep the dog where we can see it. Do not move and do not attempt to let the creature go.'

'They think the dog is Ice,' I muttered. 'They must know he can change into things. Come on let's get out of here while they're busy.'

Dragging Mr Peabody Two along with us we headed deeper into the woods, lugging our tent and other equipment with us. Fortunately our extra strength was working in our favour for a change; there was no one to accuse us of cheating or of showing off now and we almost flew through the woods, whizzing round silver birch trunks and ploughing through brambles and patches of nettles.

'This is good fun,' Jun Mo said as he pushed his way through some shrubbery, 'I feel like a Chieftain Tank.'

I followed him, chuckling to myself despite the worry that we were being pursued by gun toting special-forces, because Jun Mo did look like a tank with his stocky body and broad shoulders driving forwards over the rough terrain.

'Have you any idea where we're going?' Charlotte panted beside me as we raced along. 'Did you recognise the area where Ice said he had to meet up with his group?'

'Not exactly, but as long as we head south west, I'm sure Ice will let us know precisely where he needs to go when we get nearer.'

'Are we going to run all the way?' she groaned. 'We may have extra energy, but I think I've got a blister coming on my heel.'

'If I remember rightly, there's a station a couple

of miles from here. We could get a train some of the way at least,' I replied.

Soon the woods gave way to a main road and we had to slow to a walk to avoid drawing attention to ourselves. Mr Peabody looked a little strange in the assortment of clothes he was wearing; Charlotte's sweatshirt, my spare trousers and a pair of my old trainers, but fortunately no one seemed to be taking any notice of us and I didn't think we looked so strange that anyone would report having seen us.

It wasn't long before we came to the small branch station. There were only two other people in sight, sitting on the benches. One was a young man wearing headphones and the other an elderly lady reading a book. I was pretty sure they weren't anything to do with the Space Agency. After checking in the waiting room and ticket office for armed men, we stood on the concrete platform and looked at the route map to see what trains were heading south.

'Where is your group?' I asked Ice as he leaned against the ticket office wall beside me. 'Where should we go?'

Ice studied the map for a while then waved a green tipped finger in a general south westerly direction. 'Near here,' he said.

I looked at the train times and noticed there was a train going that way in the next few minutes. Handing the five pound note back to Jun Mo that the real Mr Peabody had refused as payment for breakfast, I asked if he and Charlotte were okay about staying with us.

'We don't all need to go,' I said. 'Your parents must be worried stiff.'

'I'm staying,' Jun Mo said.

'Me too,' Charlotte nodded, 'but I think I should just text my mum to let her know I'm okay. Can I borrow your 'phone Will?'

I handed Charlotte the 'phone while Jun Mo went off to the ticket office to buy our tickets. Ice stood beside me looking rather tired and I wondered if it was because he was in the body of an elderly man, or because his inner core was running out of energy…energy we were busy using up. Looking into his watery blue eyes I thought I detected a hint of desperation. Perhaps he didn't believe he'd ever join up with his group. I also wondered if the energy that made up Ice could die just like any other living thing and the thought made me a bit scared for him.

Charlotte handed me back the 'phone and I saw that she was looking at Ice too.

'He looks tired, doesn't he?' she said.

I was about to reply when the 'phone in my hand rang. Glancing down at the illuminated screen I saw that it was Luke calling again.

'What happened?' he asked in a low whisper. 'You cut me off in mid sentence.'

'The Space Agency men turned up,' I told him. 'And they had armed special-forces with them. They certainly aren't messing around in their hunt for Ice.'

'Did you get away okay?'

'Yes,' I said, 'But Ice seems to be getting really tired. I think he's running out of energy.'

'Look, that's what I was trying to tell you,' Luke said in the same urgent whisper. 'I wouldn't believe any of this except for the way these guys are acting, so listen up. You know that dirty ice stuff you put into those freezer bags? Well I didn't know what it was. I knew you were up to something but I couldn't work out what. Anyway, I'm sorry I made you put it in your cokes and drink it. What's it done to you anyway? Are you sick little bro'?'

'We're not sick, we've just got all this extra energy, like I was trying to tell you earlier. It's really weird, but we can run faster, we're stronger and cleverer too.'

'That wouldn't be difficult,' Luke said, still in a whisper, though I could tell he was teasing again. He never could resist a dig at me whenever he could get away with it. 'That's the only reason you managed to get one over on me the other day, isn't it? I thought you'd progressed in your fighting abilities a bit fast.'

In the distance I could hear the wailing of emergency vehicle sirens and lifted my head to listen. It seemed to be getting louder.

'Got to go, Luke,' I said as Charlotte and Jun Mo grabbed Ice between them and started off down the platform out of sight of the road. 'I think we might have been spotted.'

'I just wanted to tell you…' Luke continued. But I pressed the 'end call' button and hurried to join Charlotte and Jun Mo at the end of the platform.

'What are we going to do?' Charlotte asked as she pulled Ice into a gap behind a soft drinks machine.

'They'll find us here for sure; there's nowhere to hide.'

We were saved having to make the decision to hide or run, by the distant rumbling of an arriving train. The sirens from the emergency vehicles had receded again into the distance – or else they were simply being drowned out by the noise of the train, it was difficult to tell.

The train seemed to take an age to appear round a bend in the track and even longer to slow to a creaking halt. The moment the automatic doors slid open we stepped on board, pulling a bewildered and exhausted Ice behind us.

Charlotte sank onto a blue patterned seat and Jun Mo, Ice and I followed suit, keeping our heads down and our eyes firmly away from the car park end of the platform. We waited while the doors hissed softly shut and then closed our eyes and sighed deeply in relief.

The train jolted and lurched into motion and then we were rolling out of the station, heading generally south, hoping to find Ice's friends before he ran completely out of energy or we were found by the men from the agency…whichever happened first.

At length I opened my eyes again and stared out of the window, watching as narrow back gardens and bramble strewn embankments and then open fields sped by as the train clickety- clicked comfortably along the track. I ran my eyes over my companions, wondering if we were heading away from danger or into it. I felt responsible for them somehow as if this adventure was all my fault.

Charlotte still had her eyes closed, Ice was looking out of the window with a sort of tired fascination at what he was seeing and Jun Mo was staring fixedly at something further down the carriage.

I was about to follow his gaze when my mobile rang again and I pressed it to my ear.

'What is it this time Luke?' I said.

'I keep trying to tell you,' he hissed. 'The ice you put in those freezer bags and hid behind the frozen peas...I didn't throw it away.'

I felt my insides give a lurch that had nothing to do with the swaying of the train. 'What did you say?'

'I didn't know what it was, but I knew you were up to something, so I crept down in the night and shook it out of those bags.'

'What did you do with it?'

'I put it in an empty ice cream carton and nipped over to my mate Craig's place. It's in his mum's freezer hidden behind their frozen veg.'

'Crickey!' I said softly, glancing over to where Ice was slumped against the seat opposite me. 'I wish you'd told me earlier. We need that ice, Luke, and now we're heading away from you and away from the very stuff that Ice might need to keep him alive.'

The Muggers

20

The train continued its southerly journey passing more houses and towns and school playing fields, all the time taking us further and further from the part of Ice that might make the difference to his survival.

'Where are you then?' Luke hissed, still keeping his voice to a whisper. I pictured him locked in his room with an armed guard standing outside.

'Is anyone listening in? Can anyone hear what I tell you?' I asked suspiciously.

'Nah, they've given up watching me too closely. I pretended to drink the rest of the beer and get paralytic, so they've left me lying on my bed. The others are still under close guard in the sitting room downstairs.'

'Look, we need that ice, Luke,' I said. 'We're on a train heading south. We're planning to stay on it until Ice tells us to get off. He's got to meet up with some other…er.'

'Aliens?' Luke put in helpfully as I struggled for the right word.

'Well, yeah, I suppose so,' I said.

'Why are you helping him?' Luke asked. 'These goons seem to think he's some sort of major threat to humanity. Has he got you brainwashed or something?'

I looked across at Ice again. His head had sagged onto his chest and he seemed to have gone thin and very slightly transparent, as if some of his life force was ebbing away into the seat behind him.

'No, we're here because we chose to help him. He's harmless, Luke, he wouldn't hurt a fly. He says he needs to join up with some others of his kind to complete some sort of mission.'

'And you're certain that mission doesn't include the annihilation of the human race, little bro'?' Luke pressed.

I was surprised and rather impressed that Luke actually cared about the rest of the human race. I'd always thought he was out for a good time without much of a thought for anyone else. Maybe he had a sensitive side after all, I thought.

'He says his kind have been coming here since the Earth was able to support life,' I said firmly, 'The human race wouldn't be here at all if he hadn't wanted it to survive; I'm sure of it.'

'Okay, I'll take your word for it. Whatever your mate is, he sounds a lot better mannered than the thugs that are guarding me now. I don't like them one little bit, they show no respect, bro, no respect at all.'

'Can you give them the slip?' I asked.

Luke gave a snort. 'I've been sneaking out of this room since I could walk,' he said. 'What do you want me to do?'

'When Ice tells us to get off the train, I'll text you with the name of the station we've arrived at. If you can get out of the house without those men seeing you, go and get the ice and bring it to us. Make sure it's in something leak proof because if it melts on the way I should think we can still use the melt water. We'll find somewhere to hide until you get to wherever it is we're going. We'll sort out our next move after that, but keep your 'phone on you or we'll never make contact.'

'Will do squib,' he said.

I glanced up to see that Charlotte and Jun Mo were watching me closely.

'Big brother's coming to help us then?' Charlotte said and I realised they had been listening to my end of the conversation and didn't need much filling in.

'He's got the ice?' Jun Mo asked. 'I thought he threw it away.'

'Yeah, he was just being Luke, trying to annoy me. He knew we were trying to hide the stuff so he thought it would be funny to hide it from us. That's Luke,' I said, 'but at least one piece of the space ice is still intact.'

I heard the swish of the interconnecting door between the long carriages behind me, but didn't look round.

'Uh oh,' Jun Mo said quietly.

I turned sharply then, my stomach knotting, expecting to see the grey suited agency men or the armed police officers. Instead I saw a group of older teenagers; Luke's age or older, maybe in their early twenties, all wearing hoodies and baseball caps. I wasn't sure which was worse; official thugs or these bad looking dudes.

We all looked fixedly out of the window, trying not to draw attention to ourselves as they made their way noisily down the carriage. We heard them stop a few seats behind us and I closed my eyes, willing them to pass us by. But they never quite got to us, because someone else had drawn their attention.

'Give us yer handbag,' I heard one of the youths snarl.

'Go away or I shall call a guard,' an older woman's voice retorted. I wondered if it could be the woman I'd seen waiting for the train with us back at the station. We'd been in such a hurry to get on board without being spotted that I hadn't noticed her get on and sit a few rows away from us.

'Just give it 'ere you old bag,' I heard someone say.

'Certainly not,' the woman's replied. 'You boys should go out and get proper jobs instead of taking other people's things.'

'Oh no,' Charlotte groaned anxiously as she hunched in her seat. 'Why doesn't she just give them the bag?'

'She's a tough lady,' Jun Mo said, rolling his eyes as if to show he wished she wasn't. 'What are we going to do?'

I glanced at Mr Peabody Two and saw that he was wavering slightly in his seat as if his molecules were having trouble staying clumped together in human form. 'I don't know,' I said, clenching my hands into nervous fists. 'We've got problems of our own – look at Ice, it's as though he's melting.'

We all stared at Ice, hoping he wasn't suddenly going to disappear altogether and then there was a scream from behind us and we heard a scuffle. I felt hot and cold all over at the same time and felt a tightness in my chest as I leapt to my feet. I was going to have to do something about what was happening to the woman and somehow save Ice at the same time...but everything seemed to be slipping wildly out of my control.

Standing in the swaying corridor Jun Mo and I turned to face the bullies who were crowding round the protesting woman. I realised with a sinking feeling that there were five of them. And they were huge.

'Let her go,' I said. It was an effort just to stand there and keep my voice from cracking, so I gripped the metal rail above the nearest seat and tried not to look terrified.

The man nearest to me looked up in surprise and then smiled nastily. 'What you gonna to do about it then?' he asked.

I stared back at him, noticing the hard face and mean eyes showing beneath his baseball cap. All of a sudden I wasn't scared at all. Something inside me seemed to weld all my trembling limbs together and a strange calmness took over. I knew Jun Mo was at my elbow and I planted my feet squarely on the tilting floor and said again, 'Let her go.'

The man nudged one of his mates and they all

looked round, their eyes on me and Jun Mo now.

'And I said, what you gonna do about it, *little* boy?' he said.

'Your mummies know you're out do they?' said another of the yobs with a laugh.

I was a bit fed up being called 'little'. Luke liked to call me 'little bro' just to annoy me, though with him it was sometimes friendliness. But there was no friendly intention here, that was for sure. And at thirteen years of age I was pretty tall for my age, not little at all. Even Jun Mo who only came up to my shoulder was bigger inside than all five of those bullies put together.

'We were just appealing to your better nature,' I said, 'but you probably don't have one so I'll tell you once more; leave the lady alone.'

'Don't dear, it's not worth it,' the woman said to me, struggling to her feet and trying to take a step towards us.

One of the bullies pushed her hard and sent her flying against one of the seats. I heard a bang as her head hit the carriage window and she slumped down holding a hand to her face. Enraged, Jun Mo put his head down and charged the offender, knocking him clean off his feet and the one who had been taunting me aimed a swing at his back as he passed. I leapt forwards and grabbed his arm before he could land the punch and held on as he tried to shake me loose. One of the others grabbed the back of my summer shirt and tried to yank me backwards and suddenly there were fists flying everywhere.

For the first time in my life I knew what it must feel like when a soldier goes into battle. All thoughts other than survival were swept from my brain and I fended off the blows left, right and centre and landed a few well timed punches myself. I heard Charlotte give a warriors yell and join the fray and then there were grunts of pain and the cracking of a few noses and it was only when the blows stopped landing on and all around me that I dared look up and see what was what.

The five yobs were lying face down on the carriage floor. Jun Mo was sitting on top of two of them holding them down with his solid body weight. Charlotte had another pinned down with his arm twisted behind his back, there seemed to be one lying in a bloody heap beneath me and the fifth was being held in place with the point of the woman's umbrella. A couple of long flick knives gleamed on the floor a little way off under one of the seats and I felt my newly found battle lust begin to crumble.

'Crickey,' I said in my best Australian accent, 'They were carrying knives like Crocodile Dundee!'

The woman smiled rather shakily at me. 'If you children have modelled yourselves on Crocodile Dundee, then I am eternally grateful to the Australians. I shall call the police on my mobile 'phone and they will be waiting at the next station to take these gentlemen into custody. I really can't thank you enough.'

'The police!' Charlotte exclaimed, looking horrified, 'oh no.'

The woman looked at her, puzzled. 'The police will have to be called. What else can we do with our prisoners, my dear?'

'Can't we just tie them up and leave them here?' Charlotte suggested.

'This isn't the wild west, dear,' The woman said. 'We have to call the authorities. And then we will have to go with them to the police station and give statements about what happened.'

'No police,' Jun Mo said, shaking his head.

The woman peered intently at each of us in turn then seemed to come to a decision. She nodded sharply. 'Very well, I shall enlist the help of some other passengers. I'm sure we are not the only people on this train to have had some trouble from these gentlemen. Perhaps we can keep them here for one more stop after you children get off.'

We nodded, and she smiled. 'I don't know what you are running from, but you were heroes today and I will repay your bravery by trusting that you have not done anything too serious to make you afraid of our wonderful police force.'

She took the point of her umbrella from the man she had been guarding and I realised he was unconscious anyway. I wondered who had knocked him out; the whole incident had been such a blur.

'Keep an eye on them,' she said as she made her way to the interconnecting door, 'I will be back shortly with some help.'

'Thank you very much,' I called. 'We and our friend Mr Peabody are grateful to you.'

'Who?' She said in a puzzled voice as she turned back to answer me and paused to scan the length of the train behind us. 'There's no one else in this carriage my dear, except the three of you, me and these gentlemen lying in a bloody heap on the floor.'

The Search for Ice

21

As soon as she had gone, I craned my neck round to look at the seats where we'd been sitting with Mr Peabody Two only moments before the fight had begun. The man beneath me moaned and tried to shift my weight off him, sensing a chance to free himself.

'Keep still,' I said, 'Or you will be very sorry.'

To my amazement he stopped wriggling instantly and lay still. I wondered what had really happened during those blurry minutes of the fight to make him so afraid of me.

'Mr Peabody's gone,' Charlotte said from her uncomfortable position kneeling by the man she had pinned face down by his heavily tattooed wrist. 'I can't see him anywhere.'

I was pleased to notice that she hadn't referred to Ice by his own name. These thugs we were restraining were probably listening to everything we were saying and would pass any information they had about us to the police when they were eventually called.

'We have to find him before we get to the next station,' I said, scanning the empty seats for a hint of his outline. 'If we don't get off there we'll spend the rest of the day giving statements about what happened here.'

At that moment the woman returned followed by three burly passengers from further down the train.

'I don't know how you did it,' said one of the men as he relieved Charlotte of her prisoner. 'These yobs came through our carriage earlier looking like trouble and a couple of the passengers were forced to hand over their valuables to them.'

'We caught them off guard I think,' Charlotte said as she stood up and brushed the dust from the knees of her jeans. 'What are you going to do with them?'

'This lady has called the police and they will be waiting at the next stop but one,' said the second man. 'She has asked us to pretend we never saw you for some reason. Personally I think you all deserve a medal.'

I stood up gratefully as one of the passengers took charge of my prisoner. When they rolled him over I saw that there was blood crusting round the side of his nose.

'I think the fight broke out between these gentlemen themselves over the sharing of the spoils,' the woman we had defended said aloud. 'I was in this carriage all alone and I saw them start fighting with my own eyes.'

'Thank you,' we all said as Jun Mo climbed off his two prisoners to join us.

'Don't mention it,' said the woman with a twinkle in her eye. 'It has been a very eventful journey. And thanks to you, I still have my handbag.'

Jun Mo, Charlotte and I left the woman and the other three passengers with the groaning prisoners and began to examine every seat in the compartment for a sign of Ice. But he had simply vanished. The train started slowing down for the next station and we were almost despairing of ever finding him in time.

'Ice, where are you?' I hissed as I returned to the seat where he had last been seen. I picked up one of two old newspapers that someone had left lying on the seat, hoping to see some sign of him and then my hand froze on the paper. The paper felt strange; sort of solid and heavy and *alive* and the realisation came to me that this might be Ice. And under the other paper I found Charlotte's top and my spare shoes and trousers all lying in a heap.

The train drew into a station and Jun Mo and Charlotte looked at me, wide eyed with dismay.

'What are we going to do?' Charlotte wailed, 'We can't leave him behind after all we've been through.'

'I don't think we will have to,' I said, winking as we gathered all our equipment off the seats and I stowed the newspaper carefully into the top of my rucksack. 'I think he's still with us.'

When the train had pulled out, we stared around us at the small country station we had alighted at. It was small but very neat and tidy, with a white fence and flowering plants in pots. It was quite hot in the midday sun.

'Where are we?' Jun Mo asked. 'What's that sign say...Little Caulton?'

I shrugged as I sat myself down on a nearby bench and pulled the newspaper out of my rucksack, 'Never heard of it.'

'What are you doing?' Charlotte asked. 'Where is Ice?'

'Hopefully Ice is right here,' I said, spreading the paper out on my lap. 'This newspaper is made from paper and paper is made from wood pulp and wood pulp comes from trees. Trees are natural, and I think Ice is being this newspaper. Here...' I held it out for Charlotte and Jun Mo to feel. 'See? It doesn't feel quite right.'

Charlotte took the newspaper from me and felt it carefully. 'Do you know, I think you're right.' She said. 'Ice, is that you?'

'Newspapers can't talk,' Jun Mo pointed out and Charlotte glared at him.

'How is he going to be able to show us the way then?' she said indignantly. 'We have no idea where to go from here unless he can tell us.'

'You going to 'phone Luke?' Jun Mo asked, changing the subject. 'Tell him the name of this station?'

'I'm not sure,' I said. 'The trouble is this might not be the right station at all. Ice didn't tell us to get off here; we were kind of thrown off by circumstances, weren't we? If I tell Luke to come here we might be long gone by the time he arrives - if we can think of a way to let Ice communicate with us of course.'

We sat and looked at each other. We were tired and very thirsty and Jun Mo had a large bruise coming on his cheek bone where one of the thugs had landed a blow on him.

'What are we going to do?' Charlotte asked in a small voice. 'We've come so far and now we're stuck.'

I took the paper back and rested it against my chest while I thought of what we could do. 'We can't stay here, that's for sure,' I said. 'As soon as the train gets to the next station they'll come looking for us, no matter what that lady might or might not say.'

And then Ice solved the problem for us. The newspaper began to shimmer in the heat and droop against me and before I had time to pull it away the molecules that made up the paper were merging into my cotton shirt, much as Ice had done that first day in the shed when he had become my school shirt and hung there looking silly. Only this time I was wearing the shirt and I could feel Ice's energy coursing through the fabric, round my back and chest and down to the edges of my short sleeves.

The newspaper had gone and I felt surrounded by something cool, flimsy and invisible. Slowly I got to my feet, holding my arms out and doing a twirl for Charlotte and Jun Mo, who poked at my shirt and laughed.

'You are wearing Ice,' Charlotte said, giggling, 'this year's fashion statement from Little Caulton.'

'Are we in the right place?' I asked, looking down at my chest. 'You are going to have to communicate with us, Ice.'

And to my astonishment, my shirt tugged my arm into the air as if it was doing it all by itself and positioned my hand on the pocket of my rucksack. Beneath my hand I felt my mobile 'phone and I hooked it out of the pocket.

'I think he wants me to make the call to Luke,' I said with a grin.

'Why doesn't he simply become you instead of your stupid shirt?' Charlotte asked, 'then he could talk to us properly.'

'I think he's running out of energy. Remember how tired he looked as Mr Peabody? He was having trouble holding his molecules together. Perhaps the human form is too much for him now so he has to become more simple objects like the newspaper or this cotton shirt,' I said, texting the name of the station to Luke's mobile number as I spoke. 'Let's hope that when Luke gets to us with the rest of the ice, Ice will feel stronger again.'

'Where now?' I asked, looking down at my chest again. I did feel remarkably silly talking to my own shirt, but there was nothing else for it.

Ice hoisted me to my feet. It felt as if someone had put their arms round me from behind and had lifted me up from under my arm pits.

'Looks like he has a plan,' I said, trying not to laugh. It felt so weird to be guided like this, but I knew we had to get out of the station as quickly as possible so I grabbed up my share of the equipment and hoisted it onto my shoulder. Ice's shirt molecules separated under the weight of the rucksack, in the same way that an inflatable airbed or toy might go flat at the point of pressure, making the rest of the shirt blow up slightly round my back and chest, but it wasn't a horrible sensation, just really odd.

Jun Mo and Charlotte scooped up the rest of the stuff between them and I allowed myself to be guided along by Ice who was pushing against my back to make me walk forwards. And in this strange fashion we walked out of the station, stopping briefly at a vending machine to get some supplies and along a grass verge which ran between a road and a housing estate full of identical looking red brick houses.

'It's very built up here isn't it?' Charlotte commented as we trudged along. 'I though as we went south it would get more countrified.'

'They build all the time,' Jun Mo said. 'Soon England will look like a big concrete city.'

Eventually the road took us out of the suburbs and the houses fell away to be replaced by scrubby moor land. Charlotte stopped to rub her feet where a blister had formed on her heel and then when she thought she could walk again I felt Ice guiding me sideways, away from the road into low heather and gorse covered terrain that looked quite difficult to walk through. There was a severe looking barbed wire fence running along the edge of it, but I could see a place where it had sagged a bit and we could climb over.

'How are we going to explain to Luke where to meet us?' Charlotte grumbled as she stumbled along. 'We're in the middle of nowhere.'

'We need some sort of marker for him to make for,' I agreed, looking round.

'What's that?' Jun Mo said, stopping so suddenly that I nearly fell over him.

We looked up and saw a hill in the distance, with a water tower perched on the summit. It shined white in the afternoon sun; a big concrete tank on stilts overlooking the surrounding countryside like a great brooding bird of prey.

'There's our marker,' I said, fumbling for my 'phone. I dialled Luke's number and got him on the first ring. 'Hi Luke, have you managed to escape yet?' I said.

'No probs,' he replied. 'I was down that drainpipe and through the hole in next door's fence before they even knew I was gone. I've got that ice stuff from Craig's freezer and we're both on the train right now, heading your way.'

'Brilliant!' I said. 'When you get off you'll have to turn left and walk beside the main road until you get right out of the built up area. We're in a load of gorse and open countryside, but there's a big white water tower on the hill ahead of us. We'll wait for you there.'

'Uh oh,' Luke said ominously into the 'phone.

'What's the matter?'

'The train's just pulling into Little Caulton and I can see uniformed police officers patrolling the platform and a couple of suits that look like agency goons.'

'What are you going to do?'

'Blag it, little bro',' he replied with a laugh, 'Blag, blag, blag…it's what I do best.'

Tanks and Missiles

22

After walking for another twenty minutes the water tower didn't seem any closer, so we sat ourselves down on a couple of rocks we'd spotted sticking out of the heather and settled down for a short rest. Charlotte took off her trainer and inspected her heel and Jun Mo handed round cans of cola and some crisps he'd bought at the station vending machine.

I felt very exposed as we drank and munched the crisps. There was no real cover anywhere nearby and I worried that we weren't far enough from Little Caulton station if the police decided to start searching for us from there. It wouldn't be long, I knew for the authorities to link the incident on the train with their search for the three missing children and the supposed terror threat from space.

It was then that we heard the tank. I know we all heard it at the same time because Charlotte dropped her trainer as her head shot up and Jun Mo stopped chewing to listen at exactly the same moment that I detected the low rumble in the distance.

'What was that?' Charlotte asked fearfully.

'Sounds like a tank,' Jun Mo said through a mouthful of crisps.

I remembered the wire fence we'd scrambled over to get off the road and felt the hairs on the back of my neck stand up.

'What's that red flag flying over there?' Charlotte continued. 'I didn't see it earlier.'

'I don't want to alarm you guys but I think we may have wandered into a military training area,' I said fearfully, rolling into a crouch and staring off in the direction of the noise. 'I think we'd better get the heck out of here.'

'Wait for me!' Charlotte wailed as Jun Mo and I quickly packed up the drinks and empty crisp bags. 'I haven't got my shoe on yet.'

The tank was visible now; having risen like a great metal monster from a dip in the ground and it was moving in our direction. The speed of it was astonishing; for such a cumbersome looking machine it was travelling easily over the rough terrain, gliding over gorse and heather and jutting stones as if they were as smooth as a tarmac road. And running in a crouched position alongside the monster were a group of camouflage-clad soldiers...all carrying alarming looking machine guns.

'Come on, Charlotte!' I cried as she struggled to force her trainer over her blistered and swollen foot. 'We have to go now!'

'I can't get it on,' She cried, 'It just won't go.'

Staring about me in panic, I tried to think what to do. The tank was still coming in our general direction, but was slightly to one side of us and the soldiers seemed to be looking straight ahead and not at the three of us still crouched by the small outcrop of rocks…for the moment. I knew Charlotte wouldn't get very far in bare feet; the gorse was prickly and there were thistles and small sharp stones hidden in the heather which would tear her feet to shreds.

'We have to hide real quick,' Jun Mo yelled over the roar. 'They'll see us any second!'

'There is nowhere to hide,' I yelled back.

And then it felt as if some giant hand was lifting me by the scruff of my neck and hurling me forwards. Arms outspread and legs flailing I cannoned into Jun Mo and Charlotte, knocking them backwards into the soft heather as I landed full on top of them.

'Hey!' Jun Mo protested from beneath me.

'What's going on?' Charlotte squealed to one side of me. She was half buried by Jun Mo and me, but she wriggled sideways and lay in the heather as if she was too exhausted to make much of a fuss.

My shirt, which was snagged on a sprig of greenery, seemed to soften and spread out sideways like a blob of butter melting in a saucepan. It ran wetly over my head and then flowed over Charlotte and Jun Mo until we were all covered by a thin blanket of fine silken heather.

'It's Ice,' I hissed, trying not to giggle hysterically. I felt rather like I had been cocooned by a large damp flannel and was still shocked by the speed at which Ice had reacted to the danger of the advancing tank and soldiers.

'What's he doing?' Charlotte panted forlornly. 'I can hardly breathe.'

'He's camouflaging us,' Jun Mo said in a muffled voice. 'Ice is a camouflage net.'

We lifted our heads and peered out through the thinly woven blanket of heather. I found I could see the thundering tank and the soldiers as they advanced on our position.

'What if the tank runs over us?' Charlotte said fearfully.

'We'll just have to hope it doesn't,' I said.

The tank was quite close now and I could feel the vibrations of the huge machine running through the ground beneath me causing my heart to beat faster and my breath to come in short gasps. The noise was almost unbearable and I reached up and put my hands over my ears.

'Soldiers!' Jun Mo warned, at least I assume that's what he said, because his speech was drowned out by the grating and tearing of the tank as it passed us by a short distance to our right. A group of soldiers ran in a half crouch almost on top of us, their weapons held in front; faces covered with camouflage paint. A polished black boot landed a hair's breadth from my face and I heard Charlotte stifle a gasp. Another boot thumped down nearby and I realised the soldiers were jumping over the rocks above us and just clearing our hiding place as we lay hidden on the lee side of the outcrop.

'Enemy to the left!' a yell like a war cry shrieked in my ears, and the soldiers dived to the left of our position, spreading themselves across the low lying ground and pointing their weapons at wherever their supposed enemy lay.

A huge explosion nearby rent the air in two, rocking the ground beneath us. I heard Charlotte scream and wondered if I'd screamed too, or if it had been Jun Mo. I buried my face in the rough scratchy ground and scrunched my eyes tightly closed. I could smell some sort of charge filling the air with acrid smoke. This, I decided, was as close to war as I ever wanted to come. It was hot and loud and stinking - and this was just a training exercise, not even the real thing.

The sudden quiet after the explosion had died away seemed eerie and I was about to lift my head out of the dirt when the soldiers nearby opened fire with their automatic weapons. The noise was unbelievably terrifying and my whole body shook with the shock of it. Above my head and across my back and legs I felt Ice quiver and wondered if he was afraid, or whether he'd been hurt.

The machine guns continued to rattle out their bullets and I sank deeper into the ground. Another explosion rent the air and small stones and earth cascaded down over us as we clung together, too terrified to move, hoping that the camouflage cloak over our heads would keep us from the worst of the deluge.

It seemed an age before the machine gun fire moved away from our position and the explosions erupted further and further away from where we lay. We heard the soldiers move off with shouted orders from their officer and the ground gradually became still.

After a while, I lifted my head out of my arms and peered around me. The simulated battle had moved away further to the east of us and had disappeared over a rise in the ground. Sitting up cautiously I pulled the thin blanket of heather off my head and turned to check that both Charlotte and Jun Mo were unharmed.

'That,' Charlotte said shakily as she sat up, 'was awesome.' She looked from me to Jun Mo who was still lying with his face covered. 'You okay Jun Mo?'

He groaned and slowly lifted his head, nodding. The bruise he'd received during the fight with the thugs on the train seemed even more purple now against his ashen face.

'A big rock hit me,' he said, rubbing the back of his head, 'even with Ice protecting us.'

We gathered the net of heather together into a pile and inspected it closely. In places it was singed from the explosions and there were ragged holes here and there. I reminded myself uneasily that this wasn't just a blanket; it was Ice's body.

'Are you okay Ice?' Charlotte asked anxiously.

'Blankets can't talk,' Jun Mo said, and grinned as Charlotte scowled at him.

'What are we going to do?' I asked. 'We won't know if Ice is injured unless he takes on human form, and I don't think he has the energy to do that now.'

'I hope Luke gets here soon,' Charlotte agreed, nodding. 'When Ice gets the rest of his energy he can tell us if he's hurt and what he's planning to do.'

'Luke had better watch out,' Jun Mo pointed out 'He's got no Ice to protect him on this military training ground; it's very dangerous here.'

'You aren't kidding,' Charlotte said, picking up her trainer and making another attempt to put it on her injured foot. 'We could have been killed.'

'I'm sure they were only using blank ammunition,' I said with more confidence than I felt. The gun fire and explosions had sounded pretty realistic, though I was sure that live ammunition wasn't used on training exercises.

'Don't you believe it,' Jun Mo said, rubbing at his head. 'I looked up some stuff about joining the army on the internet a few months ago, and in some army training grounds live firing takes place almost every day of the year!'

'I think you should 'phone Luke and tell him to be very careful,' Charlotte said with a shiver.

'If he managed to evade the goons at the station,' I said, rummaging in my rucksack for the 'phone and dialling Luke's number quickly. He answered on the first ring.

'Hiya little bro',' he said, panting.

'How are you doing?' I asked him, 'Are you anywhere near the military training grounds?'

'Is that what this place is?' he said with a laugh. 'I wondered what was with the barbed wire and explosions in the distance. How did you get inside?

Craig and me, we're having trouble following your instructions with this great tall fence in the way.'

'There's a place where the fence is down,' I said, 'but they're doing training exercises so it's really dangerous in here. How did you get away from the agency guys at the train station anyway?'

'I just talked my way through, squib. Look, the battery is running low on my mobile so we should keep our little chats nice and short. Tell me, are you still aiming for the water tower?'

'Yes.'

'Okay, we'll get there as soon as we can.'

I put the mobile back in the rucksack and started to roll up the heather sheet that was Ice, so I could carry him more easily. I did it as gently as I could, but I could have sworn I heard him groan.

'I'm sorry Ice,' I said as I laid him across the top of my rucksack. 'I'm sorry you've got hurt while you were protecting us. We'll do our best to get you to your friends as soon as we can.'

Charlotte reached out to pat him encouragingly, but she quickly drew back her hand with a look of concern on her face. 'Oh no, I think he's really badly hurt,' she said showing us her hand, which had come away from Ice covered in sticky plant sap. 'I think he's bleeding.'

And it was true. Where the tears in the heather net were their worst, a thin green sap was leaking out and trickling down the side of my rucksack. I looked at my own hands and found they were sticky too, from where I'd rolled him up.

'Do you think he's going to die?' Jun Mo asked.

I shook my head. 'I hope not,' I said, 'because if he does it will be all our fault for meddling with the meteorite in the first place.'

'Don't die, Ice,' Charlotte pleaded as she at last managed to get her foot back into her trainer and we were ready to set off once more. 'Please just try to hang on.'

Reinforcements

23

By the time we reached the water tower Charlotte was limping badly and Jun Mo was looking quite pale beneath his black eye and bruised head. I felt a bit guilty that I wasn't injured too, but I supposed it was just as well as someone had to be fit and thinking clearly.

Grateful to be at our destination at last, we dumped all the gear in a heap under one of the metal legs of the tower. There were shrubs here at the top of the hill and small trees which screened us from prying eyes, but we could see the patchy moor land stretching out for miles below us. The soldiers had moved off or perhaps even completed their manoeuvres and the explosions and gunfire had finally died away.

Charlotte sat down and pulled off her shoe again and I grimaced at the sight of the bloody, pulpy mess on the back of her heel.

'I don't know how you walked with that,' I said.

'Didn't have much choice, did I?' she replied, inspecting the damage carefully, and I realised she had changed since we'd first discovered Ice. She was less scared and far more determined.

'You are very quiet Jun Mo,' I said as I sat down and leaned my back against the metal strut. 'Are you okay?'

'Got a headache,' he said, rubbing the back of his head. 'Lucky I've got Ice's energy or it might be worse.'

Looking at him, I realised that he and Charlotte were filthy. Both had dirt on their clothes and faces from the earlier tussle on the floor of the train, and mud and cinders from the explosions. Charlotte's clothes were torn in places and both she and Jun Mo had bits of heather and other plant material in their hair. I realised I must look much the same, almost as if we were in camouflage dress...not so different to the heather matting that was lying across the top of my rucksack.

Thinking of Ice, I lifted the roll of heather netting off the top of my rucksack and laid him carefully at the foot of the metal leg. He lay there looking limp and green and I suddenly realised that we wouldn't know if he was alive or dead while he was imitating a plant.

'He's kind of shrivelled,' Charlotte said, touching the heather with her grubby green fingertip. 'Maybe he needs some water, I mean he hasn't got roots or anything to suck water up from the ground so perhaps we should water him, like a house plant.'

'I've only got the rest of the fizzy stuff we got at the station,' I said, rummaging in my bag to double check that the bottle of orange squash I'd brought from home had all gone. I located it and shook it upside down but it was quite empty. 'Here,' I said, handing Charlotte the remainder of the bottle of cola. 'It's all I've got. Do you think it will be better than nothing?'

'I'm not sure,' she said, 'we don't want to make him worse.'

We were still contemplating the dilemma of whether to pour cola over the heather matting that was Ice or not, when Jun Mo gave a shout, 'Look! Over there by the road...see?'

We looked up to see two figures far in the distance, picking their way through the tangles of dark green gorse and pink heather.

'It's Luke and Craig,' I said excitedly. 'They're nearly here!' I turned to Ice and patted him gently. 'You're going to be okay Ice. Luke is here with the rest of your missing energy.'

Ice didn't give any indication that he had heard or understood, but then I thought, he was mimicking the DNA of a clump of plant material and as Jun Mo had pointed out, plants could neither see nor speak.

We watched hopefully as Luke and his friend Craig trudged towards us, eventually coming to the small incline at the foot of the hill and then disappearing from sight amongst the trees. We waited for them to re emerge from the trees nearby after they'd climbed the hill and we waited - and then waited some more.

'Where did they go?' Charlotte whispered at last.

'I don't know,' I whispered back, knowing that the same thought had occurred to both of us – that Luke and Craig had somehow been intercepted in the trees and that danger lurked close by.

'We'd better go look,' Jun Mo said quietly, 'They've been too long.'

'I'll wait here with Ice,' Charlotte said, 'I can't get my shoe back on over this wound anyway, it's just too painful and swollen.'

Jun Mo and I helped Charlotte move Ice and all our belongings behind the bushes at the base of the metal strut so they wouldn't be immediately visible to anyone who came up the hill and out of the trees, then we gave Charlotte the thumbs up sign and we left her smiling anxiously after us as we slipped silently down into the tree line.

The trees on the hill were mostly small stunted oaks and a few spindly silver birch saplings. Beneath these lay a tangle of ferns and other greenery that tried to snag our feet and scratch our legs, but our extra strength enabled us to keep ploughing our way through the obstacles until we were in the depths of the cover again.

It wasn't a big hill and soon we heard male voices somewhere ahead of us and we ducked behind a squat rhododendron bush on the edge of a small open space to watch for Luke and Craig - or whoever it might be.

I held my breath as two grey suited figures loomed out of the trees into a small clearing dragging a protesting Luke behind them.

'This isn't a game, son,' one of the men said, giving Luke a shove so that he almost fell into the clearing. He just managed to regain his footing as he lurched forwards and he turned to face them. But I had seen, in that fleeting second before he turned that my tough brother Luke was scared and in the next instant I saw why. Luke's friend Craig was half carried into the clearing by two more of the agency men. His face was bleeding and he was being dragged by his armpits as if he was half unconscious.

'You can't do this sort of thing to ordinary law abiding people,' Luke protested. 'This isn't some third world backwater where you can rough people up and get away with it.'

'You and your friend were caught trespassing on military training land, lad,' said the same man again in an even but ominous voice. 'Anything could have happened to you – all sorts of accidents befall people who stumble into a danger zone. You could be blown up by mortars, shot dead by automatic weapons, burned by exploding shells. Why even your own mother wouldn't recognise you after an accident like that.'

'You won't get away with it,' Luke said bravely.

But I knew my big brother and I knew he wasn't at all sure of himself now. And he had every right to be scared – these men knew their business and they were obviously used to getting their own way.

The men holding Craig dropped him roughly onto the ground and he sprawled there and lay still. One of the men pulled a hand gun out of a shoulder holster and pointed it at Craig's outstretched hand.

'He'll soon wake up when we blow his fingers off,' said the man nastily. 'If you know where your brother is hiding then I suggest you tell us.'

My heart was beating so loudly I was sure Jun Mo must be able to hear it, and a cold hand seemed to encircle my chest, squeezing the breath out of me. He was going to do it, I knew it, and Luke seemed to sense that the man wasn't bluffing because he tried reasoning with them again, buying time.

'Look, I'll tell you everything I know, but it isn't much,' he started.

'Go on, son.'

'My brother said he was heading south. Craig and I cut through the military training grounds so you wouldn't follow,' Luke said. 'Craig and I said we'd meet them down by the coast but we don't know where exactly.'

'Why did they want you to meet up with them?' the man asked.

I was glad Luke hadn't told them about the water tower, though now it seemed such an obvious land mark I was afraid they'd guess it even without help from my brother.

Luke hesitated and the man holding the gun pulled back the safety catch with a clunk that vibrated round the clearing.

'They er...needed us to bring them some er...supplies,' Luke said quickly.

'What sort of supplies? And what do you know about the thing they've got with them?'

'I only know what you and your friends told me; that there was something inside the meteorite that is supposed to have landed in our garden.'

The man stared at Luke for what seemed like an age and Jun Mo and I held our breath.

'Take off that back pack and show me what's inside,' the man said eventually.

Luke slid the back pack off his shoulder and opened the top flap, showing the man from a distance.

'There's nothing much in here,' Luke said, his voice quavering as the other man levelled the gun at Craig's outstretched fingers. 'Just some food and drink for my brother and his friends.'

'Take it out.'

Luke took a couple of bags of crisps out of the bag and held them out.

'Drop them on the ground,' instructed the man.

Luke dropped them onto the ground and stared round him as if looking for an escape route.

'What else?' said the man.

Luke looked for all the world like a cornered rabbit and I knew that he was trying to stall; trying desperately not to let the man know he had the very thing that the men were searching for, right there in his bag.

'Empty it!' the man shouted suddenly and I almost gasped, but clamped a hand over my mouth to stop the sound escaping.

Luke tipped the rucksack upside down and a vacuum flask fell out onto the leaf mould with a soft plop.

'What's in the flask?' said the man.

'Just some water for my brother and his friends,' Luke said in a voice that was cracking with tension.

'Open the top and bring it here,' the man instructed.

I could see from the close attention all the men were paying to the exchange that they had guessed the contents of the flask. I watched as Luke unscrewed the top of the flask and held it out to the man nearest him. The man took the flask and tipped a small quantity of the dirty melted ice water into the lid of the flask.

'Rather dirty water for drinking,' the man commented; a grin lighting up his harsh face.

He screwed the lid back on the flask and tucked it carefully into an inside pocket. 'Okay lad, that's all we wanted. We'll take you and your friend back to the base for further questioning, but you won't be harmed, you have my word.'

Luke's shoulders sagged and I knew he was feeling like he'd failed us. But he'd had no choice; it had been his mate's fingers, or a creature he didn't know and who for all he knew was here to destroy us anyway. I didn't blame him one bit, but I knew that without that extra energy, Ice and his mission were doomed.

Alien Energy

24

Jun Mo and I watched as Craig was carried away and Luke turned to be led off through the trees. I heard Jun Mo give a sigh beside me and knew he felt as I did, that we had failed Ice badly.

Then suddenly Luke did something strange. We watched as he stopped dead, gave a loud groan and doubled over, clutching his stomach. It looked like he'd been poisoned, or maybe the men had roughed him up more badly than we'd realised. I nearly broke cover to go to him as he staggered sideways and crashed into some bushes, but Jun Mo tugged me down. The men leading Luke turned and looked at him in horror.

'What's wrong lad? You didn't drink any of that stuff did you?' one of the men said gruffly.

'No, I didn't touch it,' Luke said in a voice raw with agony as he writhed and groaned on the ground.

'Hold out your hands!' barked the man who had been reasoning with Luke earlier. 'Let me see them.'

'He's looking for green fingers,' Jun Mo whispered in my ear. I realised my friend was still holding me back, obviously afraid I'd go rushing to Luke's assistance.

We watched as Luke clawed his way to his feet and held out his badly shaking hands. From our position we couldn't see if they were green or not, but I wouldn't have put it past Luke to want to sample the super strength I told him the melted ice would give him.

Jun Mo and I held our breath, wondering if the sickness was all an act and Luke would try giving them the slip. If he was as strong and fast as Charlotte, Jun Mo and I were, he might think he'd got a chance to evade his captors.

'Okay son, it looks like you're telling the truth,' the man was saying.

'Not green then,' Jun Mo whispered with a puzzled frown, 'he must have been careful not to touch the ice when he moved it.'

Luke made a sudden retching sound and turned back into the bushes again.

'He must really be ill,' I hissed anxiously, trying to get to my feet.

Jun Mo pulled me back down into our hiding place. 'The men will take care of him,' he said firmly. 'No point giving us away too.'

The men stood in a group nearby seeming at a loss while Luke edged further into the bushes, retching as he went. All that could be seen of him was his blonde head and the sound of him being very sick.

After a while, Luke came back looking much

better. He was standing upright now and was wiping the back of his hand across his mouth.

'You alright now lad?' asked the leading man, holding out a handkerchief so that Luke could wipe his face and hands.

'Yeah I think so,' muttered Luke. 'Must have been something I ate.'

'Okay, well you'll still have to come back with us for further questioning. You can show us on a map what part of the coast your brother and his friends planned to meet up with you.'

Breathing a sigh of relief, I watched as Luke meekly allowed the men to march him away, the rustling of their passage through the stunted trees dying away as they left the hill and returned to the open heather strewn training grounds below.

'Come on,' Jun Mo said, breaking cover at last. 'We'd better get back and tell Charlotte what happened.'

'Not until I've had a look at the place Luke was sick,' I said.

'Ugh!' Jun Mo exclaimed, 'What you want to do that for?'

'Because,' I said with the beginnings of a hopeful smile, 'Luke has never been upset by anything he ate in his whole life. He's been known to eat a gigantic roast dinner followed by an enormous curry in the space of a couple of hours. I've seen him pick the mould off a cheese and eat it whole and he's never ever sick...not unless he drinks too much beer anyway, and he didn't say it was something he'd drunk did he?'

Jun Mo shrugged, 'He seemed pretty sick to me.'

'Come on, let's look anyway,' I said.

Even though we knew the men had gone, we crept through the trees carefully, trying not to make any noise. The thinly wooded hill had returned to its natural state now that the bombing down on the range was over and the agency men had departed, taking Luke and Craig with them. Birds hopped from branch to branch over our heads and a squirrel raced across the small clearing and dived for the nearest tree trunk as we appeared.

The undergrowth was quite dense where Luke had disappeared to be sick. There were brambles and ferns and a few stinging nettles and it was hard to see exactly where he'd been. I peered under the ferns and poked about with the toe of my shoe and suddenly I saw what I'd been hoping to find. There, lying hidden at the base of a tangle of vegetation was a slender back pack, with a long tube leading from one end; a drinking nozzle at its tip.

'Brilliant!' I said with a laugh, 'Luke must have had this hidden under his clothes all along. The flask was just a decoy!'

'What is it?' Jun Mo asked.

'It's one of those drinks bags people take on walking or cycling expeditions,' I explained. 'There's a soft plastic container inside that you fill with water, then you wear it on your back so your hands are free and you drink the water from this tube.'

'You think Luke had this under his shirt?'

'Must have,' I beamed. 'He obviously realised he

might get caught, so he put dirty water in the flask and the real stuff in here. I knew he wasn't really sick the minute he said it was something he ate. Hey Jun Mo! This means we can save Ice after all!'

We picked the water bag up and headed back up the hill to where Charlotte was waiting anxiously for us at the base of the tower.

'Where have you been?' she demanded. 'I was beginning to think you'd both been caught. I don't know what I would have done if I'd been left here with Ice all on my own.'

'Luke and Craig have been caught,' I told her. 'We thought Luke had given the agency men Ice's energy in a flask but he tricked them. I'm pretty sure it's in here.' I held up the bag to show Charlotte, but she didn't look impressed.

'I just hope you're not too late. Ice has just been lying there leaking green sap the whole time.'

We clustered round the base of the tower where the heather matting was lying on some short scrubby grass. All around the mat there were green patches where the sap had leaked out of Ice's wounds into the ground.

I poked Ice gently with one green tipped finger and the matting twitched slightly beneath my hand.

'He's still alive then,' I said. 'But how do we give him the ice water? Should I pour it over him or what?'

'I don't think that's a good idea,' Charlotte said, 'Suppose it just soaks into the ground? We won't be able to get it back again once it's spilt.'

'Does the water bag have an opening?' Jun Mo asked, peering at the bag in my hands. 'Could we push the heather mat into the bag of ice water? Then none can spill out.'

I pulled the plastic bag out of the back pack and found a circular cap where Luke must have posted the lumps of ice stuff before they melted. Presumably he'd taken no chances with the space ice and worn gloves as he can't have touched it, or he'd have the green fingers just like Charlotte and me. It occurred to me that the Space Agency didn't know everything about Ice or they would have realised Luke wouldn't have had green fingers just from drinking the ice water. It seemed you actually had to touch it like Charlotte and I had. 'We could probably push the matting in here,' I said dubiously. 'But what if we drown him by mistake?'

We sat around contemplating the best course of action. None of us was keen to risk killing Ice by either drowning him or wasting his precious energy by pouring it over him. The clear plastic bag was lying across my knees and I stared at it gloomily.

'What's that?' Charlotte said suddenly, poking the bag with her green tipped finger.

'What?' I asked.

'That,' Charlotte said.

I looked at the bag more closely and realised that the dirty ice water inside wasn't just liquid; there was something pale and shiny floating in the water.

'It looks like Ice did when we first saw him in the pool in the shed,' Jun Mo said excitedly.

'It's the rest of Ice's energy!' Charlotte squealed. 'Of course, why didn't we realise that? It's not just some sort of energy tonic for Ice to drink to make him feel better...this is part of the original Ice before we broke him up by chipping bits off him.'

'This might even be the real Ice,' I said, staring at the bag. 'I mean this might be the stronger part of him, the better part or even the more important part.'

'Do you think that wasn't even a real meteorite that landed on your shed at all?' Charlotte said suddenly. 'That Space Agency man, Temoc, told us it was only the dust and the rocky trail of a comet that formed a meteor shower. Surely any real ice would have burned off when it entered the earth's atmosphere? Do you think the stuff we thought was dirty looking ice could have been some sort of alien material made up from the carbon hydrogen and oxygen atoms Mr Peabody was going on about... but in the form of a sort of space egg with Ice's molecules floating inside it?'

'You know, I think you could be right. The puddle in the crater didn't form until it rained through the hole in the shed roof,' I said, amazed that we hadn't sussed this before. 'What if the meteorite didn't just *contain* an alien life form, what if it *was* the life form...a sort of space egg, as Charlotte says? When we removed part of it and put it in those freezer bags the rest of the meteorite just melted away into the shed floor didn't it? All those atoms and molecules were just waiting for the opportunity to become something - and then it rained and the creature was able to absorb some of the water like a sponge filling out, and then it saw us and copied my DNA and Ice was born. Only all this time he's only been a fraction of himself, which is what he was trying to explain to us back at the Scout camp.'

'And we just assumed we'd found a real meteorite,' Jun Mo agreed, nodding. 'That's probably why Ice and his kind arrive during a meteor shower. If anyone sees anything strange they think it's to do with the meteor display in the sky!'

We all stared at the pale floaty thing in the bag.

'What if this is the more dangerous part of Ice?' Charlotte put in. 'What if this is the part that makes the Space Agency men so afraid?'

We sat and thought about this for a few minutes. The men weren't trying to find us for nothing. Whatever it was they were afraid of had made it worth roughing up Luke and his friend Craig and the strength of the police task force they had enlisted had seemed quite formidable.

'What are we going to do?' Charlotte said.

'I don't know,' I replied. 'But I do know that Ice promised he wouldn't hurt us to get his energy back from us and I know he protected us against the mortar explosions by shielding us with his own body. He wouldn't have done that if he was bad, would he?'

'Maybe he just wants us to keep helping him,' Jun Mo warned.

'I just feel in my bones that he's harmless,' I said, shaking my head. 'Mum always taught us not to judge a book by its cover; in other words not to be prejudiced by how things or people appear on the outside. You can tell a person's worth by their deeds, and so far Ice hasn't shown us anything other than friendship and protection.'

'So you think we should let that energy stuff out of the bag?' Charlotte asked.

I nodded slowly. 'We all believed Ice was worth saving when we first met him, didn't we? Otherwise we wouldn't be here now, hiding out by a water tower in the middle of an army training ground, hungry, dirty and thirsty, with our parents probably worried sick about us and the police and special agency forces on our trail.'

Charlotte giggled, 'You make it sound pretty awful,' she said. 'But I think you're right. I like Ice and I don't want him to die.'

'Jun Mo?' I asked.

'I like Ice too,' he agreed. 'Open the bag.'

Out of Balance

25

Jun Mo and Charlotte watched while I slowly unscrewed the flat cap of the drinking bag. When the cap was hanging free by its plastic safety thread, we peered inside at the strange transparent mass that lay inside like a blob of clear jelly.

'How do we get it out?' Charlotte asked hesitantly.

'I think we should let Ice sort that out,' I said, and I laid the open bag on top of the heather matting.

We all watched as the bag lay there for a moment without anything happening. Then, very slowly, the mass of jelly oozed towards the opening of the bag and slid out onto the clump of heather that was Ice.

We held our breath as the jelly settled out over the heather, seeming to absorb it into its midst and then suddenly the whole thing began to tremble very slightly, then it shook and quaked a little more until it was leaping and seething with what looked for all the world like the joy of simply being alive.

Jun Mo laughed and leaned a little closer and in that split second the mass reached out a jelly-like finger and touched him on his face. Jun Mo reeled back with the shock of it and I wondered if it had felt as ice cold as Ice's finger had done when I'd reached out my hand to touch him that very first day in the shed.

The mass wobbled and twitched before our eyes and then a second Jun Mo emerged from within and sat looking at us with interest from beneath the leg of the water tower.

'Crikey,' Jun Mo said in his Korean version of an Australian accent. 'Better put some strides on, mate.'

The new Ice cocked his head onto one side as if considering what Jun Mo had said, then he reached out and touched Jun Mo's trousered leg. Within seconds Jun Mo Two was wearing an exact replica of the real Jun Mo's trousers.

'Wicked!' Charlotte said with a giggle.

The new Ice looked at Charlotte and something strange began to happen to his head.

'What's he doing?' Charlotte yelped, as two pointed horns shot out over Jun Mo Two's ears.

Ice made a horrible face and I realised that he was trying to look...well, wicked. 'We'd better watch what we say around the new Ice,' I warned. 'He understands what we're saying, or he thinks he does.' I turned to Ice. 'We don't want you to look mean or wicked,' I said. 'Charlotte meant that she thought it was cool, you making your own trousers like that.'

'Oh,' said Ice in a perfect imitation of Jun Mo's voice, 'I look cool, yeah?'

'Lose the horns, Ice,' I said. 'We need to talk.'

The horns disappeared into Ice's head and he sat there looking rather dejected.

'We need to know more about you,' I began. 'We have to understand *exactly* what it is you've come here for and where you need to go. We got the idea while you were Mr Peabody that your kind are the seeds of life on this planet...but life is doing fine here, isn't it? So why do you still need to come?'

'Human life is doing fine, yeah,' Ice agreed. 'But nature is out of balance: no balance, no life.'

'So what exactly is out of balance?' I pressed him, realising that if we were going to continue helping him we had to know for sure that it was the right thing to do.

'Humans take resources from the Earth. They must learn to give back, to take no more than they need and then replant and restock,' Ice said. 'People cut down forests and leave no habitat for other species. More importantly, without trees there would be no oxygen and no food. This planet is provided with food and oxygen through photosynthesis; the process by which plants manufacture their own food from sunlight.'

'We know all that Ice,' Charlotte said uncomfortably. 'We've done photosynthesis at school and we've been taught about conservation and it's really boring.'

'Not boring,' Ice said, shaking his Jun Mo-like head. 'It's important you understand. You've heard of the 'greenhouse effect'? Too much pollution results in a build up of 'greenhouse gases' and a change to your world's climate. Trees can help by soaking up the carbon dioxide. Fewer trees mean fewer people can survive; no trees...no people will survive.'

'Are you here to be a tree?' asked Jun Mo in disbelief. 'Is that what all this about? Just flippin' trees?'

'Blimey,' I said, 'you mean those meteorites or whatever it is you guys are, keep coming to Earth to reseed the trees on our planet?'

'What are the agency men so scared of then?' Jun Mo demanded. 'Are you telling me they carry guns to stop *trees* growing?'

'We can be many things,' Ice said with a smile. 'Trees are just one of them. They know we can be whatever we need to be and they would like to capture us and use our energy for their own ends.'

'What sort of ends?' I asked curiously.

'Military probably,' Ice answered with a shrug, 'which could be very dangerous to the rest of the world. Or possibly medical. Imagine how much of your Earth money a government institution could make if they could grow new body parts or whole people to order. It sounds amazing but our energy could be badly misused in the wrong hands.'

'But it *is* just trees this time?' Charlotte checked, 'You're not going to do anything amazing or dangerous that might make a difference to mankind's existence are you?'

Ice looked at her as if she was crazy. 'Yes, I am doing something amazing and dangerous and I hope to make a BIG difference to mankind's existence. I'm going to make trees...and if I can find the others we will make vast forests and keep you humans alive.'

We sat in silence, contemplating this new intelligent Ice. Then I glanced down at my fingertips and gave a short laugh. The clue had been there all along, Ice was green, like nature itself, like everything we humans labelled as pure and environmentally friendly and he had touched us and now we were green too. Mum liked to say people who were good with plants had 'green fingers'. Well ours were certainly green. Like the knights of old, we were here to help make the world a better and safer place to live. Crikey.

Jun Mo was still looking disappointed though, as if he thought that Ice's mission wasn't half as exciting as he'd thought it was going to be.

'What did you think we were going to do?' I asked with a grin. 'Put Ice in a bicycle basket and cycle him through the sky to meet with his comrades as they landed in a spaceship?'

'Don't know,' Jun Mo said, shrugging. 'But I didn't think it would be trees. I thought we were going to save the world at least!'

'You will be saving the world,' Ice insisted. 'You are the generation who must put things right before it is too late. You can start by cutting down on the emissions: by walking to school instead of going in the car, by recycling your rubbish, or turning the TV off at the switch instead of leaving it on standby.'

'If that's all we need to do, then why bother with extra trees?' Jun Mo asked somewhat huffily, kicking at a stone with his shoe. I could see he wasn't sure about this new, rather intense Ice.

But Ice wasn't going to be put off by Jun Mo's obvious disappointment. They stared at one another; two Jun Mo's looking like a couple of young bulls about to lock horns.

'Breathing is pretty important, huh?' Ice said at last. 'And having food to eat?'

'I'm breathing fine right now,' Jun Mo said. 'And there's plenty of food. It comes from supermarkets.'

'Only because there are still just enough trees,' Ice explained patiently. 'Forests are the lungs of the world. Also, supermarkets get food from farmers and farmers grow crops that need rain to make them grow; and forests encourage rainfall.'

They stared at one another for a moment and Charlotte and I held our breath, wondering who would back down first.

It was Jun Mo. 'Okay, okay,' our friend said, holding up his hands in defeat. 'I understand. We don't want you caught and used for the wrong purpose so we'll help you with your mission – even if it is just to make trees.'

Ice grinned. 'We are not yet at the proper destination. We need to travel further.'

'It won't be easy,' Charlotte cautioned, with a sigh of relief. 'Everyone will be on the lookout for us now.'

'We go across country,' Ice said, getting to his feet and then stopping to look down at his bare toes. 'But I need shoes if I'm to travel as Jun Mo.'

'Can't you make some?' Charlotte asked.

Ice shook his head. 'Your shoes are made from manmade material,' he said. 'I can only replicate cells that are alive or have once been part of a living thing.'

'Told you so!' Jun Mo said with a smug look, and I remembered he'd come up with that theory when we'd first let Ice out of the shed.

'Just as well I gathered these up from the train when you disappeared after being Mr Peabody,' I said, digging in my rucksack for my old trainers that I'd lent to Mr Peabody Two way back at the camp site; 'Genuine plastic through and through!'

I handed them to Ice who put them on. They were several sizes too big for Jun Mo's feet, but at least they'd stop Ice's feet from being torn to shreds on the rough ground.

'Can you copy a top?' Charlotte asked, staring at Ice's bare chest.

'No need,' I said, handing him the baggy sweatshirt Charlotte had lent Ice when he was being Mr Peabody Two, 'he can wear this again.'

Ice pulled the top over his head without any further instructions and I thought again how quickly he learned everything. We only had to tell him something once and he sort of sucked the information in and held on to it even though he was in a different body again.

We were about to set off when Charlotte sank down and put her head in her hands. 'You'll have to leave me behind,' she said. 'My foot is too painful to walk on, and I'll hold you up.'

Ice got down on his hands and knees and inspected Charlotte's heel. The blister had long since broken and the raw skin was peeling away round the edges of a large weeping sore. Reaching out, Ice touched the centre of the wound with his finger tip. Charlotte flinched away from his touch, but then her eyes grew wide and round.

'Ooh, the pain has gone!' she exclaimed.

Ice removed his finger and we all stared at Charlotte's heel. The skin was a healthy pink, smooth and unbroken. Ice had healed her with his energy.

'Blimey,' I said quietly. 'Now that was really cool.'

And I was beginning to realise at last quite how powerful Ice could be and why those agency men were so desperate to find him.

The Mission

26

After Charlotte had put her trainers back on and we'd hoisted the equipment onto our shoulders, the three of us set off after Ice who was striding ahead setting a brisk pace down the other side of the hill, across the heather strewn plain. We had to climb awkwardly over a section of tall wire fencing to get out of the military training area and soon found ourselves walking through neatly tended fields and farmland. Ice was moving so quickly even in the slopping shoes that there was no way any of us would have kept up with him if it hadn't been for the extra energy we'd absorbed when we'd drunk his ice water.

We walked for another three hours, until the sun sank behind the horizon and the blue sky was streaked with the pink of the setting sun. We'd passed many small wooded areas and I thought more than once that it looked to me as if we had plenty of trees; but then we skirted round the outskirts of several sprawling towns where there were none. Even in the open countryside we passed several ugly gashes on the landscape and I remembered from lessons at school that hundreds of new landfill sites and several incinerators were scheduled to be built in the south of the country to dispose of the mounting problem of household and industrial waste. I wondered where on earth they were going to be put and what would happen to the green rolling landscapes of England then.

Ice was slowing now and I wondered if we'd have the chance to rest and eat. My stomach was rumbling, reminding me that I hadn't had a proper meal since Mr Peabody's bacon and eggs at breakfast time. Darkness was falling in earnest now and I was looking forward to the end of this adventure, when I heard the sound. The others had obviously heard it too; a low beating sound, which grew louder and louder until we stopped in the shelter of some outbuildings near a farm and stared up at the purple sky.

Helicopters: three or four of them swept out over the nearby woods, their headlights gleaming like the eyes of giant insects, spotlights sweeping back and forth across the dark open fields. One of the clattering machines hovered over our position and I wondered if they had the infra red cameras which could detect body heat, but then it swept away to join the others and I let out a long slow breath.

'Someone must have seen us,' I hissed to Ice as we cowered against the wall of the crumbling farm building which was still warm from the rays of the dying sun and which had probably shielded us from the sensors. 'The agency men must have found out that Luke's water wasn't you and they're hunting for us again. If someone has reported seeing us, I don't know how we're going to escape this time.'

We had a short stop in a nearby barn and munched on the last of the sweets I had hidden at the bottom of my bag for emergencies. There was clean tasting water in a trough in the corner of the field and we scooped it up in our hands and sipped as much as our stomachs could hold in one go.

Ice was agitated at the stop and paced about as we rested, but even with our extra energy, Jun Mo, Charlotte and I were nearing the end of our reserves.

'I must go,' Ice said, going to the door of the barn and peering up at the dark sky. 'I have to meet up with the others.'

'Can't they make the trees without you?' Jun Mo asked irritably from where he was slumped on a pile of hay bales. 'It not all our fault you're keeping them waiting; your meteorite must have been way off course, wasn't it?'

'We travel in from wherever we land,' Ice said, still peering out at the sky. 'In past times we seeded where we fell, but now we have to be more precise. We become birds, small mammals, whatever it takes to get to the meeting place.'

'So what happens if all of you don't make it?' Charlotte asked. 'Do you just abort the mission and go home?'

Ice turned his deep brown Jun Mo eyes on her and sighed. 'There is no way back from where we came,' he said softly. 'We have to get to the meeting place or we soak away into the ground when our energy runs out...like you saw me do on the train when I was being your Mr Peabody.'

'That's ridiculous!' Charlotte said. 'Why can't the others make a smaller amount of trees without you? Surely some trees are better than no trees at all?'

'You could make a tree all of your own in the corner of this field,' I suggested. 'Then at least you'd still be alive.'

Ice actually laughed, even though what we were really talking about was his death if he didn't meet with the others soon. 'You don't understand,' he said. 'To become a single tree would be a waste of resources. This was not the mission.'

He stopped pacing and stared at each one of us in turn. He was the most deadly serious we had ever seen him. 'Do you think one dinosaur would have survived on its own? Could one human being have started the whole of the human race alone? Can one soldier win a war? No. It requires many of one species for it to take root and grow and blossom. To make an impact on the Earth, you need an invasion.'

Jun Mo caught my eye and I knew he was thinking the same thing I was; were the agency people right after all in wanting to hunt Ice and his kind down? But it was too late now. I didn't think we could stop Ice even if we wanted to and the thought sent a shiver down my spine. He was so incredibly strong since Luke had brought the rest of his energy, much stronger than any of us. In fact, as I watched

Ice start to pace again I realised that he was pretty well invincible.

Charlotte was looking at me now with a sort of half worried, half questioning look on her face. It would be totally dark soon and we were in the middle of nowhere, with a creature who had just admitted his kind were here in invasion force to bring significant changes to our planet. We also knew that a special agency was trying desperately to locate him and despite our gut feelings that Ice was harmless, I hoped to goodness that we were right.

As soon as Ice went to peer out of the doorway yet again, Charlotte, Jun Mo and I huddled together on the hay bales for a whispered consultation.

'You do think it really is just trees he's going to make?' Jun Mo said anxiously. 'I *knew* trees were too boring for a mission like this. What if he's really going to do something else?'

'I believe in Ice,' Charlotte insisted. 'I've heard a lot about greenhouse gases and I saw a programme which said that the polar ice caps are melting already because of global warming.'

'We can only judge him on what we know,' I said, shrugging. 'Ice could have left us to die back there on the army training ground but he protected us with his own body, didn't he? He could have left Charlotte behind when her foot was too sore to walk on, but he healed her so she could come with us. I don't think he would do anything to harm any of us and we owe it to him to help him as best we can.'

'And he'll die, if he doesn't get to his destination,'

Charlotte reminded us with a groan. 'It's just that I'm so tired.'

Ice had heard the groan and was striding back towards us, 'We must go,' he said, looking from one of us to the other. 'Is Charlotte alright?'

'I'm very tired,' Charlotte said quietly

'We're all tired and hungry,' I said. 'You may not need sleep or food, Ice but we do. I think we should rest here for a couple of hours until we feel up to walking some more.'

Ice's Jun Mo-like eyes took on a haunted look. 'We must carry on,' he said urgently. 'The mission is to be completed soon. I can't be late.'

'We're just tired, that's all,' Charlotte said. 'We'll be alright once we've slept.'

'No time to sleep!' Ice said; clearly agitated. 'We must go now. You are my friends but if you can't keep up, I must go on alone.'

We nodded tiredly and began gathering our possessions. 'We'll come with you Ice.'

Ice smiled at us, 'I was warned that Earth was a harsh place to come,' he said. 'Those who created our energy said that humans had evolved to be cruel and untrustworthy. I did not believe this when I met with the three of you, and I see now that I was right to put my trust in you.'

'We're doing what we think is right,' Charlotte said quietly. I noticed there were tears in her eyes and in truth I felt like crying too if I could have. We believed in Ice and he had believed in us and I wanted to prove to him that he was right to put his faith in us, to prove that not all humans were cruel and untrustworthy. I just hoped we could keep up with him.

It was fully dark now, but a moon had appeared in the sky and by its silvery light we followed Ice out into the darkness and I felt a rush of adrenalin course through me. We weren't really helping this creature from outer space now I realised. He no longer needed us but we were going along as his friends. Rather like newspaper reporters we were going to be shadowing his movements, and perhaps like reporters we would get a story to tell the rest of the world...if the world survived to hear the tale.

Trudging through the moonlit night behind Ice, the three of us talked in low voices about what we thought he was going to do.

'I hope we're doing the right thing,' Jun Mo muttered as we followed in Ice's footsteps.

'We are,' I whispered back, 'we have to believe it.'

Ice ploughed across a busy main road and we waited for a lull in the traffic before following carefully across, then he headed up a side road by a pub which had light spilling from its windows and voices and laughter coming from within.

'All those people in there have no idea what's happening, do they?' Charlotte said as we hurried after Ice. 'It's just another ordinary summer's evening to them isn't it?'

'It must be nearly closing time,' I said, looking at the time on the screen of my 'phone. And then something struck me.

'Don't you think it's strange that the agency men left Luke with his 'phone?' I said suddenly. 'They must have known he'd try to contact us. And wherever we've gone, the agency and law enforcement officers have been close behind. They knew we were at the Scout camp, didn't they? And we just assumed Mr Peabody had told on us. Then they found us on the military training grounds didn't they? Don't you think it's odd that they just took Luke and Craig and didn't continue looking for us? And what about those helicopters earlier? One hovered right over us but then went away…what if we've been followed all along, tracked by my mobile 'phone?'

'Then why didn't they pick us up?' Charlotte said, hurrying to keep up as we followed Ice round a bend in the road. 'If they've known where to find us all along, then why haven't they stopped us?'

'They don't want just Ice!' Jun Mo said, realisation dawning. 'They want the rest of his kind, and we're leading them straight to them!'

I turned the 'phone off and thrust it deep into my pocket, wondering if we had in fact been followed from the very beginning. For all we knew we had been tracked since the agency guys had first been told about Jun Mo's fight with the bullies in the playground at school and their visit to his house. Maybe they'd followed him, but I thought it more likely that once they'd made the connection they had used Luke to keep tabs on us via my 'phone.

And what of Luke, I wondered? Had my brother been unknowingly used by them as he tried to help us - or was he actively helping them? I dismissed this thought as soon as it surfaced. Luke might be a lot of things, but he was my brother and I knew he would stay loyal to me. He might bully me himself, but I'd always known that he would stick up for me if need be. I sometimes wondered if my street-cred at school wasn't partly down to having Luke for an older brother.

A shout from Charlotte brought me quickly back to the present and I stopped dead in my tracks, almost bumping into Jun Mo who had halted abruptly in front of me.

'What is it?' I said, glancing round the quiet moonlit lane nervously.

'There's something up ahead of us,' Charlotte whispered. 'I saw lights, just for a moment, flickering beyond those bushes.

Ice had seen the lights too and had ducked down into a ditch that ran alongside the lane.

'Do you think it's the agency guys...or Ice's friends?' Charlotte asked.

The answer came almost immediately as a spotlight snapped on, illuminating the three of us in an arc of yellow light.

Captured

27

'Stay where you are!' commanded a harsh voice. 'Do not move.'

Lights burst on all around us and we reeled back, shielding our eyes with our hands. I tried to glance sideways to where I knew Ice was cowering in the ditch but the lights blinded me and I couldn't make him out.

Three burly uniformed men strode over to us and took each of us by an arm, leading us to where, unseen by us in the darkness, a huge dirt car park lay just off the road. The car park was filled with armoured vehicles, a white van and accompanying police vehicles. It looked like something from the set of a movie.

Jun Mo, Charlotte and I were herded over to the white van and shoved roughly into the back. Blinking, I looked round the well lit interior and felt my insides give a lurch; it looked like a hospital or a science lab inside, with bleeping machines, lines and wires and trays full of evil looking instruments.

A lab technician or possibly a doctor in a white coat climbed in behind us and closed the door.

He had on thin latex gloves, but he wasn't wearing a mask or a complete suit with face mask, so I reckoned he knew we weren't all infected with some fatal alien organism, despite what they'd tried telling Luke.

The man stared at us through the thick lenses of his glasses and shook his head of thinning hair sadly, 'You children have given us a really hard time,' he said. 'I'm going to take some blood samples from each of you and run some tests and while we're waiting for the results, I want you to tell me everything that has happened since that meteorite landed in your back garden.'

We told him everything that had happened, but when the questions turned to what Ice was planning to do next and where he was headed, I stalled for time, trying to give Ice a little longer to get to his meeting point. It was so confusing. These men were treating us as if we were traitors to our planet, but we had to believe in Ice after all he had done for us.

The doctor was beginning to get annoyed at my evasion of his questions and he turned to fill a syringe with something out of a glass vial. I was wondering if he was going to administer a truth drug or something when the doors to the van were flung open and a grey-suited man stood there staring at us with open hostility. I swallowed hard as I recognised Temoc – the Space Agency man who had first come looking for us at the school.

'What have they told you?' he barked at the doctor.

'Nothing we didn't already know, sir,' the doctor replied nervously.

'Have you administered the drugs?'

'Not yet sir.'

'Have you tried them with the instruments?'

'Not yet sir.'

'Good grief man,' Temoc said angrily. 'We haven't got all night. I want to know where the creature is headed and what it plans to do.' He turned his hostile glare onto us and I shrank back from the intensity of his gaze. 'You are a disgrace to the human race,' he told us disgustedly. 'You have been helping an enemy of our planet.'

'Ice is here to help us,' I said with more conviction than I felt. 'He wants to save the Earth from destruction.'

'You are mere children,' Temoc spat. 'You know nothing about our Earth.'

'We know that the Earth is in trouble,' I replied. 'And it will be down to our generation, with help from Ice to puts things right. But you just want Ice for your own ends.'

Temoc scowled and turned back to the doctor. 'Get me some answers and get them quickly.'

'We've only just started sir,' the doctor replied. 'But the children will talk eventually.'

I felt my stomach churn at the thought of what these men might do to us. Glancing at the others I saw that Charlotte and Jun Mo were both looking decidedly queasy too. There was nothing else for us to tell them, except the general direction Ice had been heading, and we hadn't even had a proper map at the time, only a rough drawing. What if they tortured us, I thought and there was nothing we could tell them?

The doctor went over to the van doors with Temoc, giving Charlotte, Jun Mo and me a chance for a few quick words.

'They're going to hurt us,' Jun Mo said quietly, fastening the straps of his pack back more tightly round his middle as if for security.

'I don't like these men,' Charlotte said, trembling. 'It proves we were right to choose to help Ice, he's never threatened to harm us.'

'You're right,' I said. 'They're trying to convince us that they are the good guys and Ice is the enemy but if we are judging who is good and who is bad by what they do, my vote goes to Ice. He's helped us and protected us and these people only want to hurt us. What are we going to do?'

The doctor was still at the rear door of the van having a last few words with Temoc, presumably getting instructions on how to get what they wanted out of us. Jun Mo reached round to the tray of instruments, grabbed the filled syringe and hid it behind his back.

'The good thing is that they obviously haven't found Ice,' Charlotte whispered. 'He must have changed into the hedge or something.'

The doctor finished his conversation, pulled the doors closed and was about to turn back to us when Jun Mo launched himself at the man's back, stabbing the needle into his neck. Charlotte and I quickly realised what was happening and leapt to our feet, throwing ourselves into action, holding the man down while Jun Mo used both hands to push the plunger down on the syringe. The man stopped struggling and went limp.

'Have we killed him?' Charlotte asked; her eyes wide as she stared at the crumpled body at our feet.

'Whatever we've done, it was only what he was about to do to us,' I said shakily. 'He put that stuff in the syringe, not us. And anyway, it wasn't exactly planned,' I turned to Jun Mo with the beginnings of a grin. 'Well done mate, that was quick thinking.'

'Put the lab coat on,' Charlotte said, kneeling to unbutton the man's white coat. I slipped out of my rucksack and Charlotte pulled a few things out of it and stuffed them into the smaller backpack which she was carrying. We pulled the lab coat off the man and I thrust my arms into the sleeves and stood up, fastening the front buttons with trembling fingers.

Opening the door a crack I peered out into the dark night. Now that they thought we were captive, the men were standing round in small groups, talking amongst themselves.

'Come on,' I said. 'Let's go.'

The escape plan would have failed of course. There was no way those men would have let us slip past them, even with me disguised as the doctor or whatever he was. But at the moment we opened the rear doors of the van and stepped down onto the dusty ground, a shout went up and everyone's eyes snapped towards the road. Spotlights flashed on. And there was Jun Mo Two, waving at the men with one hand while in the other he held a beautiful speckled barn owl.

'That's him!' shouted a voice and suddenly gunfire coughed from weapons all around us and every eye was on the two birds which soared up into the night sky as Jun Mo Two transformed his DNA to replicate the owl and followed it into the sanctuary of the trees.

Charlotte, Jun Mo and I dived for the bushes on the far edge of the car park to find that the car park had been built on a rise and we tumbled downwards, slipping and sliding, our clothing snagging and tearing on unseen twigs, roots and brambles. At the bottom we scrambled to our feet and hurled ourselves along unseen pathways, forcing ourselves not to notice the whipping of twigs and scratches of low lying branches in our faces as we ran for our lives.

We could hear our pursuers coming down the slope behind us now and I gritted my teeth as a branch caught in my hair almost ripping it from its roots. Charlotte and Jun Mo were panting along beside and behind me and suddenly we were hurtling downwards again, unable to see anything in the darkness, but hearing our pursuers become more distant behind us.

We picked ourselves up at the bottom of the drop and ran on for several miles, ever thankful to Ice for our extra reserves of energy and at last we came to rest where the trees parted at a narrow strip of tarmac road.

'What do we do?' I asked the others breathlessly. 'Should we try to get back to civilisation, or keep running?'

Jun Mo was leaning his back against a tree trunk and was bent double, still panting from the run. Charlotte had sunk to the ground in a crouch and was gulping in long gasping breaths.

'We've got nowhere to go,' Jun Mo said. 'We can't even go home.'

'What's that horrible smell?' Charlotte asked suddenly.

I sniffed the cool night air and wrinkled my nose, 'It smells like garbage.'

'How come there's rubbish way out here?' Jun Mo asked, holding his nose as he spoke.

'I don't know, but let's go and look,' I said. 'Come on, I have a gut feeling that this might be where Ice was heading.'

'To a garbage tip?' Charlotte exclaimed. 'What would he want to do there?'

'I don't know,' I said, shrugging. 'But he had to be heading somewhere and this is what we've found, so let's take a look.'

We crossed the road, climbed over a stile and walked along a sandy track to where the stench was coming from. On one side of us we could see moonlit farmland stretching away to the far hills with rows upon rows of crops covering the land. On the other side, behind a tall chain link fence towered a mountain of stinking, fermenting refuse.

'Ugh! I can't bear the smell,' Charlotte said,

gagging as she spoke and holding a hand over her mouth and nose. 'It's disgusting. What a terrible thing to put in the middle of this beautiful countryside.'

'It has to go somewhere, I suppose,' I said. 'Look, I'm going to climb to the top of the fence and see how far this rubbish tip goes. Are you coming?'

Jun Mo and Charlotte followed as I climbed the fence and perched precariously at the top, looking out over a vast expanse of stinking human waste products. The moonlight glinted off black refuse sacks and white plastic bags and in between there lay festering heaps of evil smelling waste.

And then we saw the owl swooping towards us through the night sky; the moonlight lighting the white tips at the end of its wings so they looked as if they had been dipped in silver.

'It's Ice!' Charlotte cried, forgetting to hold her nose for the moment as Ice alighted on the fence beside us. 'You were right Will, of all the places in the world, Ice has chosen to come here, to this horrible stinking tip.'

Invasion Earth

28

Climbing quickly down from the fence, we stood in a huddle round the owl, which hopped down to join us on the ground. It was a big bird seen close up, over 30 centimetres in height, with an intelligent looking white face and round unblinking eyes.

'Is this the place?' I asked Ice. 'Is this where you're meeting with the others?'

'Birds can't talk,' Jun Mo pointed out.

'Oh shut up Jun Mo,' Charlotte said. 'It's not a real bird, it's Ice.'

The owl hopped a few paces away, then looking back at us over its shoulder with a head that seemed to be able to swivel almost all the way round; it spread enormous wings and took to the air.

'I think he wants us to follow him,' I said, setting off after the bird. 'Come on.'

I took the small back pack from Charlotte, leaving her with only a couple of things to carry and we set off at a trot after the bird. Ice hadn't gone very far before he came down to perch on the upturned roots of a huge old tree which had probably blown down in a storm. We stopped at the tree and in the light from the moon I could see a dry hollow beneath the roots.

Ice had settled on the fallen tree's trunk and tucked his head under his wing.

'I think he's trying to tell us that this is a safe place to stop for the night,' Charlotte said.

The tent had been stowed on the outside of the rucksack we'd had to leave behind in the white van, but the hollow looked almost like a small cave. I took off the lab coat and spread it on the dry earth. Charlotte had rescued one of the sleeping bags and we unzipped it as far as it would go so that it resembled a wide padded blanket. Jun Mo produced a packet of rather grubby looking mints and we ate a couple each, sucking them slowly to relieve our parched throats. Then the three of us crawled into the space as far as we could and curled up in a heap to sleep like a litter of puppies.

I dreamt that I was at the seaside watching the fishing boats hauling in their wriggling catch; above them seagulls screeched and dived, snatching at discarded bits of silver fish. Then someone nudged me and I opened a bleary eye to find Charlotte and Jun Mo looking down at me in the early morning light.

'Can't you hear them?' Charlotte said.

'What?' I replied sleepily, pulling myself into a sitting position and almost whacking my head on the overhanging, mud encrusted roots of the tree.

'Seagulls, hundreds of them!' Jun Mo said. 'They're circling that rubbish tip we passed last night.'

Ice was nowhere to be seen, so the three of us crept back through the spindly trees and bushes we'd come through the previous night until we had a clear view of the landfill site. In the daylight it seemed even bigger than it had in the moonlight and seemed to stretch away like a gigantic festering scar on the otherwise beautiful landscape. And Jun Mo was right; there were hundreds, if not thousands, of birds. No wonder I'd heard them and dreamed about them in my sleep, I thought.

Most of the birds were seagulls, as Charlotte and Jun Mo had said, but I noticed now that there were many other types of birds too; rooks, magpies, blackbirds, jays and smaller birds like swallows and blue tits and various finches. They were calling and cawing and shrieking as if in such excitement that they couldn't contain themselves.

'What are they doing?' Jun Mo asked, his voice filled with awe.

And it was an awesome sight. The birds seemed to be swooping and diving at the garbage piled below them and at first I thought they were looking for food amongst the ripped and torn rubbish bags. But then I realised the birds were actually dropping things into the tip; and it wasn't just bird droppings. When I looked more closely I saw that each bird carried a small brown pellet in its mouth, perhaps an acorn or a chestnut or some other kind of seed.

'They're dropping things into the rubbish,' Charlotte said. 'Look, there are nuts or something falling from the sky. It's as if it's raining seeds.'

And it wasn't just the birds that were descending on the rubbish tip. For as far as we could see there were small rodents streaming from the surrounding bushes and trees; mice, rats and even squirrels scurrying under the fence, an army of small soldiers, all on the same single-minded mission.

And then we heard a shout. We stared back down the path that ran alongside the wire mesh fence to see a tall fair haired man racing towards us, his arms waving frantically.

'It's Luke!' I cried, breaking cover to go to meet him.

'Run!' Luke shouted, 'Run all of you. They've found you and they're coming to stop you!'

A shot rang out from the trees on the other side of the tarmac road we'd crossed the night before, and Luke spun round, a look of surprise on his face. Then he staggered and fell and I ran towards him, my legs feeling leaden, as if they no longer belonged to me. I reached my brother, crouched beside him and tried to turn him over, but my hand came away red with warm sticky blood. I was aware of Charlotte and Jun Mo racing towards us and I tried to shout for them to go back, but my voice was cracking with emotion and they couldn't hear me.

More shots rang out in the early morning air and suddenly the sound of firing was all around us. I hunched over my brother, trying to shield his body with mine and the firing became frenzied and constant. My whole head was ringing with the noise, but then another sound came to me; it was the furious hooting of an owl. I looked up in horror to see one bird after another falling from the sky and plunging into the tip below.

'They're killing them!' Charlotte cried desperately. 'Oh, please don't let them kill Ice.'

And suddenly I realised the men weren't aiming at us but at the birds. Enraged, I stood up and glared towards the trees from where the firing was coming. At that moment I didn't care if they shot at me or not, an ice-cold anger was spreading through my veins and like on the train, I found I understood how warriors could walk into a blazing battle without feeling fear or remorse. It was as if my senses were on hold, but despite the strangely detached feeling in my body, my brain was hatching a plan.

Pulling the mobile 'phone from my pocket, I turned it on, set it to camera mode and pressed the 'send to e mail' button, then I held the 'phone high in the air and pointed it first at Luke's bloody body, then towards the falling birds and lastly towards myself.

'If you hit me, the world will see it!' I yelled. 'You will be held accountable unless you stop shooting right now!'

And to my immense relief, the firing stopped.

I turned back to the birds, hoping to spot the owl amongst them, but to my surprise all I saw was that the birds were still falling to earth. One after the other, the birds folded back their wings and went into a steep dive, hitting the garbage below as if it were no more than water in the ocean and they were hunting fish in the world below.

'What are they doing?' I heard myself say into the void. And then I saw the owl and I understood. This was the invasion of Earth that Ice and his kind had planned from the very beginning. Each of the birds and small mammals was a ball of energy from space and they were about to bring their life force to assist a struggling planet. Ice shot out from a bush nearby and looked directly at me. I saw that he had a seed held in his beak and realised that it was the blue print for what he was about to become. He nodded his feathered head as if to say, 'everything is as it should be' and then he flew out over the fence, folded his wings tightly back against his body, jutted out his beak and accelerated towards the earth.

'Ice!' shrieked Charlotte as Ice plunged into the rubbish tip and vanished beneath the mounds of filthy black and white bags.

But for just one fleeting second before impact, I had seen Ice change into a tiny replica of the seed he had held in his beak. And I had seen a strange golden glow of energy surrounding him as the speed and precision of his impact drove both the seed and Ice Seed Two deep beneath the rubbish and safely into the depths of the earth below. And when I looked again at the frantically burrowing animals and the remaining plummeting birds, I realised that the whole tip was glittering and twinkling with tiny streaks of alien energy, which shimmered and twitched and heaved until it at last lay still.

'Ice is planted,' Jun Mo said softly into the sudden silence. 'He's done his job.'

Epilogue

Jun Mo and Charlotte told me later that I turned back towards Luke after I'd realised that Ice had got to the meeting point and carried out his mission. I had knelt beside the body of my brother with tears streaming down my cheeks, 'I'm so sorry I got you into this,' I'd said. 'Please don't be dead.'

Luke had opened one blue eye and peered up at me, 'What are you snivelling over, little 'bro? It's just my shoulder - I think they only winged me.'

I laughed with relief at finding my brother was alive, 'How did you get away from them?' I'd asked; my voice cracking.

'I realised they must be tracking you with your 'phone when they found us so easily by the water tower. Ouch that hurts,' he'd mumbled as Charlotte had pressed a spare pair of my clean socks against his shoulder wound to stop the bleeding. 'They took Craig to a hospital, but I persuaded them I might be useful to them. So they brought me along with them while they followed you, then I broke away when I realised they'd got you cornered. I had to warn you they meant business – they were talking as if they would stop at nothing to get their hands on your alien friend and his mates. I could hardly risk using the 'phone again to tell you, could I? Crikey, I think I need a beer.'

Charlotte, Jun Mo and I had all rolled our eyes. Luke obviously wasn't going to change his ways in a hurry.

The men had come then and taken Luke off to hospital on a stretcher. Jun Mo, Charlotte and I were escorted back to the white van, but this time there were no needles, just endless questions.

'You can't go around shooting innocent people,' Charlotte had said indignantly when we'd been told our parents were on their way to collect us.

'It was a stray bullet,' said Temoc, who had changed his tune since my stunt with the camera 'phone. 'We were trying to protect you children, and anyway, that boy Luke never was, and never will be innocent.'

'Why were you shooting at those poor birds anyway?' I'd asked, looking him squarely in the eye.

'We thought…well, we thought they were something else,' said Temoc evasively.

'And what do you think now?' I'd pressed.

'I think they've got away with it again,' he'd muttered with a shrug. 'But I'll be ready and waiting for them next year.'

It was all a blur to me by then. After everything that had happened and the shock of seeing Luke caught by the stray bullet, my mind had closed down and it felt as if I were watching everything through a misty curtain.

Several weeks after Ice had plunged to his fate in the landfill site, I was sitting in my bedroom staring moodily at my computer. The stupid thing didn't seem to be working properly and I wanted to contact Jun Mo and Charlotte on MSN and have another discussion about what had happened. We talked about it endlessly on the chat line.

Our parents had grounded us all for the next few weeks which seemed unfair when all we'd been doing was trying to save the world. They had been so relieved to see us again and told us how worried they'd been when no one in authority would give them permission to go home, or to tell them anything other than that we had run away and were being searched for. But we had been grounded anyway; great.

Luke and Craig were both out of hospital already and Luke was making the most of his injury. Several of the local girls had called to see if he was okay and he was certainly okay enough to stick his foot out from his resting place on the couch in the sitting room and trip me up when I went past.

All the white plastic had been removed from our house and the surrounding area and next door's dog seemed to have recovered from his experience of coming into contact with Ice and having the agency men stick needles in him, but the shed was a write off. They'd ripped it to bits while searching for Ice and taken all the parts away with them for further tests.

The computer pinged as I sat with a purring Brutus on my lap and I turned to look at it hopefully, but the screen had gone blank and er… green.

I moved the mouse around trying to get the usual blue screen to come up. I really needed to chat with Jun Mo and Charlotte to see if they were feeling as empty and drained as I was, but instead a whole load of pictures flashed up over the green background. I sat there with my mouth open as a computer animated simulation popped onto the screen and ran in front of my eyes. There was the landfill site looking very realistic but without the awful smell. Then, while a digital clock ran on in the top right hand corner of the screen, the garbage sank down. Diggers came and piled top soil over it and it sank further. The clock ran forwards and I watched as little green shoots sprang up all over the site, twisting and turning towards the computerised sunlight.

The shoots put out leaves and the stems grew into trunks and new branches and suddenly I was looking at a forest, stretching away to the horizon as far as the eye could see; and in the forest birds nested in the computerised branches and small animals scurried about on the forest floor collecting nuts and berries.

I looked at the clock in the right hand corner of the screen and saw that it had stopped. The date was 2110, over a hundred years from now, and I knew that Ice had done this. I recalled Ice sitting where I was sitting now, looking like Jun Mo Two; his hands resting on my computer as I threw things into a bag ready for our adventure and I knew that Ice had planned to tell us about his mission from that point in time.

And I knew that Ice had succeeded and that we had helped him. As the computer programme faded, I logged on to MSN, which was suddenly working just fine and sent a message to Jun Mo and Charlotte; Ice had succeeded in his mission.

I looked down at my hands and saw that my finger tips were no longer green, but I was going to be green in everything I did from now on. I wanted to carry on saving the world; I owed it to Ice and I owed it to the planet and to all the generations of people who would come after us.

Crikey!

AUTHOR'S NOTE

In July 2005, two teenagers having a sleepover alone in a house outside a small Surrey town were woken in the night by a strange crashing sound. They raced outside to find that a huge chunk of ice had fallen from the sky and had imbedded itself in the soft earth near the back door. Not knowing what to do, they eventually went back to bed, intending to investigate in the morning. The next morning all that was left of the ice was a large crater in the earth, but no sign of the ice remained.

No one knows where the ice came from.

FACT: the central part of a comet is like a large dirty snowball; a large block of ice covered in dust. As it nears the sun, this snowball starts to melt in the heat so that dust, vapours and gases are blown out in a huge trail millions of miles long called a coma.

Comets come from deep in space, swing round the sun and head off again to return years or centuries later. If Earth passes through a comet's tail the particles of dust become meteoroids and burn up in our atmosphere, which we see as a meteor shower.

The Delta Aquarids is a strong meteor shower

that peaks every year on July 28th.

Meteorites can be spectacular and can fall to Earth as a shower of small stones, a football sized rock or a huge boulder such as the one which made the Arizona meteor crater in the US that crashed to Earth about 50,000 years ago. The crater measures 1.2km (3/4 mile) across and 200m (650feet) deep!

FACT: the rhyme about the kings and queens of England is correct, although some history books leave out mention of Edward V who was the son of King Edward IV. Little Edward was only twelve years old when his father died, but in his will the King appointed his brother Richard of Gloucester as Edward's protector. Richard is rumoured to have killed his nephew (one of the princes in the Tower of London) and he took the crown for himself, becoming Richard III, nicknamed 'Dick the bad'.

Edward VIII, the present Queen Elizabeth II's uncle, is also sometimes left out because he abdicated from the throne to marry American divorcee Wallis Simpson.

FACT: All the stuff talked about by Mr Peabody is accurate, so remember MRS NERG for your GCSE's!*

FACT: There are several military training grounds in

GCSE Double Science Biology – CGP Books
GCSE/Key Stage 4 Biology – Longman Revision Guides

239

the south of England, including Minley in Surrey and Chatham in Kent. Salisbury Plain is home to the Army Training Estate (ATE) where live firing takes place on an average of 340 days a year and has facilities for armoured vehicles, artillery, engineers, infantry and aircraft.*

FACT: Tropical forests once covered more than 16 per cent of the Earth's land surface, but that figure is now less than 6 per cent. The immediate effects of deforestation are habitat loss causing the extinction of native species and soil erosion which in areas of high rainfall can result in severe flooding. Longer term consequences can include worsening of the greenhouse effect as carbon dioxide (which is normally removed by trees) builds up in the atmosphere.

*ATE & Conservation:
    www.army.mod.uk/ate/public/salisplain.htm
World Deforestation
    www.mongabay.com/deforestation